Schöningh

EinFach Englisch
Unterrichtsmodell

Series Editor: Hans Kröger

T. C. Boyle

The Tortilla Curtain

Edited by
Wiltrud Frenken,
Angela Luz and
Brigitte Prischtt

Einzelarbeit

Partnerarbeit

Gruppen-arbeit

Unterrichts-gespräch

Schreib-auftrag

Hausaufgabe

Audio-CD

filmische Präsentation

Projekt, offene Aufgabe

kreative Aufgabe

szenisches Spiel, Rollenspiel

Vorwort

Der Titel der Reihe **EinFach Englisch** verdeutlicht Zielsetzung und Programm zugleich. Einerseits soll Schülerinnen und Schülern auf einfache Art und Weise der Zugang zu klassischen, aber auch neuen literarischen Werken und Filmen ermöglicht werden, andererseits sollen Lehrerinnen und Lehrern in der Praxis erprobte Unterrichtsmodelle angeboten werden, die die wichtigsten methodisch-didaktischen Ansätze ihres Faches Englisch abdecken. Dabei sind die Modelle direkt, ohne langes Einlesen einsetzbar und stellen Unterrichtsarbeit konkret vor. Als besonders hilfreich für die Praxis haben sich dabei folgende Aspekte erwiesen, die für die Gestaltung der Reihe wesentlich sind:

- Überblick über **Figurenkonstellation**, ggf. **Filmszenen** und **Inhalt**
- **Klausuren** mit **Erwartungshorizont**
- **Arbeitsblätter, Tafelbilder** und **Leitfragen** für den Unterricht
- **Piktogramme** als Hinweise auf **Unterrichts-** und **Arbeitsformen**

Das Prinzip der **„Components“** ermöglicht darüber hinaus den variablen Einsatz der Modelle in unterschiedlich konzipierten Unterrichtsreihen. Dabei stehen Machbarkeit und Praxisnähe stets im Vordergrund.

Zum vorliegenden Modell ist im Schöningh Verlag die zugehörige Textausgabe T. C. Boyle, *The Tortilla Curtain* (Best.-Nr. 041282) erschienen.

Sprachliche Betreuung: Geoffrey Perrin

Westermann Schroedel Diesterweg Schöningh Winklers GmbH
Braunschweig, Paderborn, Darmstadt

www.schoeningh-schulbuch.de
Schöningh Verlag, Jühenplatz 1 – 3, 33098 Paderborn

Druck A 5 4 3 2 1 / Jahr 2020 19 18 17 16
Alle Drucke der Serie A sind im Unterricht parallel verwendbar.
Die letzte Zahl bezeichnet das Jahr dieses Druckes.

Umschlaggestaltung: Jennifer Kirchhof
Druck und Bindung: westermann druck GmbH, Braunschweig

ISBN 978-3-14-041278-0

Getting started

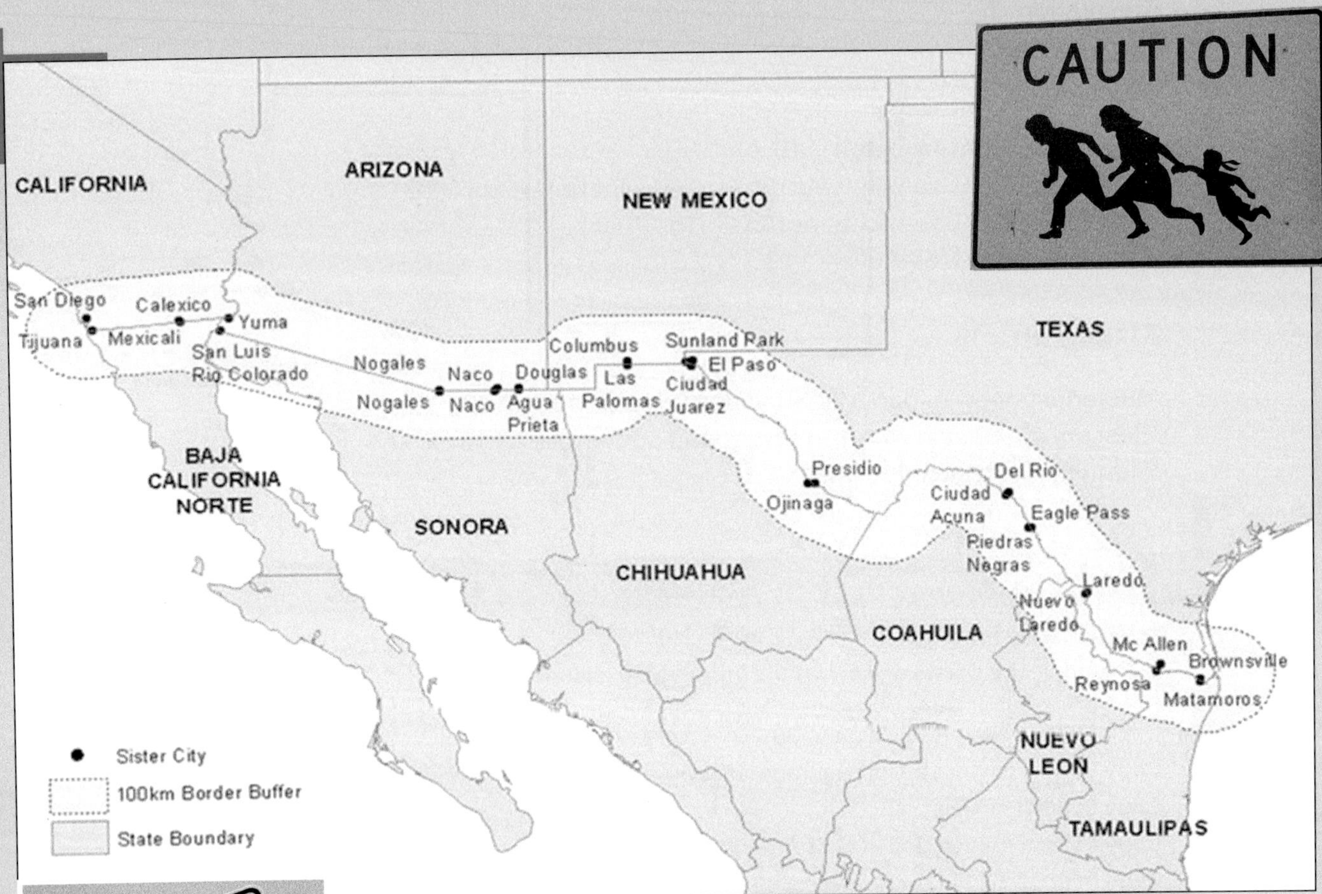

The Tortilla Curtain

The novel

The author

Tom Coraghessan Boyle was born in Peekskill (1948), a town in New York State located on the Hudson River. Boyle grew up in a working-class, Catholic family. Both his parents were alcoholics. His grandparents emigrated from Ireland and his father grew up in an orphanage. Although Boyle claims that he did not read fiction until he was eighteen, he recalls being intrigued by the newspaper stories his mother read to him. A self-proclaimed hellion who cut classes and abused drugs throughout his youth, he was much influenced by the hippie-ideals of the 1960s. After school he enrolled at the State University of New York at Potsdam intending to major in music, but "didn't have the discipline to do the practicing". He began writing as a junior at Potsdam, when he enrolled in a creative writing course. From 1964 to 1968, he was a student at Potsdam, where he majored in history and took a bevy of courses in English. While he was an undergraduate at Potsdam, Boyle took a number of history courses from Dr. Vincent J. Knapp. Following his graduation from college, Boyle taught high school English in Peekskill to avoid serving in Vietnam. During this interval he published his first short story, *"The OF & Hepatitis RR or Bust"* in *The North American Review*, and this piece won him admission to the University of Iowa Writers' Workshop. Once enrolled in the Workshop, Boyle became eligible to take classes in the English department and began work on a Ph.D. in literature. "The minute I got there," he once wrote, "I grew up. Instead of cutting classes, I sat in the front row and took notes." Although his declared speciality was the Victorian period, Boyle received his doctorate in 1977 for a collection of short fiction published two years later as *"Descent of Man, and Other Stories"*. Prior to 1988, he was relatively unknown. This was true even though he had published two books of short stories that were well received, and two novels, including a notable novel in 1982 titled *"Water Music"*. Boyle has explained that this novel "comes out of having done a Ph.D. in nineteenth-century British literature," citing the essays of John Ruskin and the novels of Charles Dickens as particular influences. His break-through came in 1988, when his third novel "*World's End*" won the PEN-Faulkner award as the best novel published that year in the United States. That novel was set in New York state. In terms of both critical and popular reception, it represented a watershed for Boyle. Recounting the tangled histories of three families living in the Hudson River valley, the narrative alternates between scenes featuring the seventeenth-century members of these clans and depictions of their descendants in the 1960s; the more recent passages also feature flashbacks to the 1920s and '30s. After receiving the prestigious award, his considerable literary talents were recognized throughout the country. And at that point, he truly became a cult writer, with a devoted group of readers. All of his books are in print, and 600,000 copies of his works are in book stores around the U.S. and internationally. Many of the motifs introduced in *"Descent of Man"* recur throughout his short fiction. One of these themes is his conviction that, beneath the technological innovations and ostensible sophistication of modern life, humans remain primitive beings who fall into one or two categories – predator or prey. Other themes in his short fiction include the tension between reason and instinct, the self-indulgent materialism that he considers endemic to consumer society and the jaded complacency that results, in his view, from media excesses. *"The Tortilla Curtain"* was published in 1995. His latest novels are *Talk Talk* (2006), *The Women* (2009), *When the Killing's Done* (2011), *San Miguel* (2012) and *The Harder They Come* (2015). Apart from many novels he has also published several collections of short stories, e.g. *If the River was Whiskey* (1989) or *Without a Hero* (1994).

His short stories regularly appear in major American magazines like *The New Yorker*. His work has been translated into more than two dozen foreign languages.
He currently lives with his wife and three children near Santa Barbara, California.

Der Inhalt

Der Roman *The Tortilla Curtain* (auf deutsch unter dem Titel *América* erschienen) spielt in einem der vielen Vororte von Los Angeles, in die sich die weißen Bewohner dieser Metropole auf der Flucht vor Verbrechen und Einwanderern und auf der Suche nach Natur zurückziehen. Der Leser trifft zwei Familien, die weißen Mossbachers, die mit ihrem Sohn in einer der neu erstellten Siedlungen für gut verdienende weiße Mittelständler leben, und die illegalen mexikanischen Einwanderer Cándido und América, die ihr erstes Kind erwarten und unter freiem Himmel kampieren.

Die Handlung setzt damit ein, dass Delaney auf einer Schnellstraße Cándido anfährt und ihn dabei verletzt. Er zahlt dem verschreckten Mexikaner 20 Dollar. Von nun an wechselt mit jedem Kapitel die Perspektive, der Leser verfolgt sowohl das Leben der Weißen als auch das Leben der Mexikaner. Beiden Paaren widerfahren zunehmend schrecklichere Dinge. Delaneys Auto wird gestohlen, beide Hunde der Familie werden von Koyoten gerissen, Kyra wird bedroht, ihr Heim wird fast von einem Feuersturm zerstört. Durch diese Ereignisse und die Gespräche mit seiner Frau und seinen Freunden und Nachbarn wird Delaney immer mehr zum Reaktionär, obwohl er sich zu Beginn des Romans selbst als liberal bezeichnet.

Die ohnehin schon unerträglichen Lebensbedingungen der Mexikaner verschlechtern sich ebenfalls ständig. Cándido leidet unter den Folgen des Autounfalls, América wird vergewaltigt, Cándido wird von einem Landsmann überfallen, sie verlieren in dem Feuersturm alle ihre Ersparnisse, ihr Baby wird blind geboren. Am Ende des Romans reißt eine riesige Schlammflut alles in die Tiefe.

Part One

1	Delaney Cándido Kenny Grissom	– Delaney hits Cándido with his car and injures him – pays him 20 dollars – takes car to dealer
2	Cándido América	– Cándido runs a high fever but recovers, has feverish dreams about Mexico – América decides to go to the labour exchange
3	Delaney Kyra Jack Jardine	– one of the Mossbachers' dogs is savaged by a coyote in their back yard – During one of the community's meetings Delaney tries to convince his neighbours of dangers of feeding wildlife – community is preoccupied with discussion about gate for estate
4	Cándido América	– Cándido remembers his relationship with his wife Resurrección, América's older sister – América tries to find work in vain – two young men, possibly Jack Jardine's son and a friend, smash up Cándido's and América's camp in the canyon
5	Delaney Kyra	– Kyra shows her favourite house, the Da Ros place, to a couple – Delaney's column about wilderness at night
6	Cándido América	– América is offered a cup of coffee by a fellow Mexican at the labour exchange – she finds a job scrubbing buddhas for a fat white man at Arroyo Blanco – Cándido also meets intrusive Mexican when looking for América

7	Delany Jack Jardine Cándido	– Delaney discusses illegals with Jack, they see Cándido at the supermarket's parking lot – Delaney decides to go for a hike, he also meets the unpleasant Mexican on the trail – returning to his car he finds it stolen
8	Cándido América	– América and Cándido buy food from her money, she can work again the next day – When she comes back from work Cándido is not there so she sets out on her own. On the way she is mugged and raped by the intrusive Mexican and his friend.

Part Two

1	Delaney K. Grissom Kyra	– Delaney buys new car – Delaney wants to go for a hike and ends up cowering behind the bushes and watching his new car – closing down the Da Ros place Kyra is threatened by the two Mexicans who have raped América
2	Cándido América	– Cándido finds a job putting up the Mossbachers' fence – he remembers other times when he was working in the USA – when returning América tells him that her money has been stolen
3	Delaney Kyra D. Flood	– meeting at D. Flood's house (he is under arrest) – members of community discuss being walled in for protection – another coyote breaks into backyard and takes other dog
4	Cándido América	– labour exchange is closed so Cándido and América set out to Canoga Park where they learn that there are no jobs – a man offers help, Cándido leaves with him
5		– one of Delaney's articles – here about coyotes
6	Kyra Delaney Neighbours	– Kyra supports idea of walling in Arroyo Blanco – Delaney is insecure about the topic – seeing a Mexican in his street he becomes aggressive
7	Cándido América	– Cándido has been mugged, all their money is gone – they must eat food from a garbage bin
8	Delaney Kyra Cándido América	– Delaney has not fought the wall – he and Kyra go shopping for Thanksgiving – Cándido gets a free turkey at the supermarket, he hopes to liven up América now. When trying to cook it he sets the canyon on fire.

Part Three

1	Delaney Kyra	– Delaney, Kyra and her mother attend D. Flood's Thanksgiving party – party is disturbed by sirens of firefighters
2	Cándido Kyra	– Cándido and América barely escape the fire, unfortunately she feels the baby coming, Cándido looks for shelter and finds the maintenance shed of Arroyo Blanco
3	Delaney Kyra Neighbours	– Arroyo Blanco must be evacuated, when the crowd sees two Mexicans climbing up the canyon they turn into a mob. They can return home, Kyra's mother has been tricked by D. Flood.
4	América Cándido	– América gives birth to a daughter, Cándido builds a kind of hut for shelter, he cooks the Mossbachers' cat in a stew

5	Delaney Kyra	– the Da Ros place is a victim of the flames – there is Spanish graffiti on Arroyo Blanco's wall
6	Cándido América	– they have lost all their money in the fire, their daughter is blind, a heavy rain sets in, Cándido is recognized and attacked by Delaney
7	Delaney Cándido	– Delaney's car is hit by a truck because he parked it wrongly – he follows Cándido on his own and wants to punish him
8	Delaney Cándido América	– Delaney finds Cándido and América in their hut and threatens them with his gun when a monstrous mudslide washes them all away, the daughter is killed, but Cándido saves Delaney from drowning

Die Charaktere

Delaney Moosbacher

Delaney lebt mit seiner zweiten Frau Kyra und seinem sechsjährigen Stiefsohn Jordan in dem neu erschlossenen Wohngebiet Arroyo Blanco weit ab vom Stadtkern von Los Angeles. Er ist als freischaffender Schriftsteller für ein Naturmagazin tätig. Delaney bezeichnet sich zunächst als liberal, was sich jedoch im Verlauf des Romans ändert.

Kyra Moosbacher

Kyra ist eine sehr erfolgreiche Immobilienmaklerin, die für den Unterhalt der Familie aufkommt. Sie betrachtet die Einwanderer aus Mexiko als Bedrohung für ihre Geschäfte.

Cándido

Der illegal eingewanderte Mexikaner Cándido (Mitte 30) lebt mit seiner Freundin América in einem Canyon in der Nähe von Arroyo Blanco. Er hat bereits mehrfach illegal in den USA gearbeitet und den Verdienst seiner Ex-Frau nach Mexiko gebracht; diesmal ist sein Ziel, genug Geld zu verdienen, um sich mit América ein Apartment leisten zu können und in den USA zu bleiben.

América

América ist 17 Jahre alt, schwanger und voller Illusionen mit Cándido in die USA gekommen, um dort ein neues Leben in einem kleinen Häuschen mit bescheidenem Wohlstand zu beginnen.

Jack Jardine

Jack ist Anwalt und ein Wortführer in Arroyo Blanco. Er fordert vehement verschärfte Sicherheitsmaßnahmen bis hin zu einer Mauer rund um die Anlage. Er hält alle Einwanderer für eine Bedrohung seines Lebensstandards. Seine politische Haltung ist äußerst reaktionär.

José Navidad

José verkörpert die Bedrohung, die die Weißen in den Mexikanern sehen. Er vergewaltigt América, stiehlt ihr Geld und wendet sich so auch gegen seine eigenen Landsleute.

Das Unterrichtsmodell

Vorüberlegungen zum Einsatz des Romans im Unterricht

Boyles Roman, erschienen 1995, eignet sich hervorragend als Schullektüre, da er sprachlich von Oberstufenkursen der Q1 und Q2 gut bewältigt werden kann. Der kontrastierende Aufbau des Romans, der die Problematik der illegalen Einwanderung von Mexikanern in die USA aus Sicht eines mexikanischen Paares, das unter menschenunwürdigen Bedingungen in einem Canyon haust, und aus Sicht eines weißen mittelständischen Paares beleuchtet, motiviert ständig zum Weiterlesen.

Die Thematik des Romans lässt sich vielfältig in das Oberstufencurriculum einbinden, z. B. im Rahmen einer Themenreihe zu *American Dream/American realities, The impact of the American Dream – then and now, Immigration and Multiculturalism*. Zudem wird der im neuen Kernlehrplan Englisch in NRW geforderten *Interkulturellen kommunikativen Kompetenz* Rechnung getragen:

- Orientierungswissen: die Schülerinnen und Schüler erweitern und festigen ihre Kenntnisse in Bezug auf die Themenfelder „The impact of the American Dream – then and now" sowie Literatur und Medien in ihrer Bedeutung für den Einzelnen und die Gesellschaft;
- Einstellungen und Bewusstheit: die Schülerinnen und Schüler werden sich fremdkultureller Werte, Normen und Verhaltensweisen bewusst und begegnen ihnen mit Toleranz; Begegnung und Wahrnehmung kultureller Stereotypen und deren Reflexion; Erkennen und Verstehen kulturspezifischer Konventionen;
- Verstehen und Handeln: in der Auseinandersetzung mit den historisch, politisch, sozial und kulturell geprägten Lebensumständen von ethnischen Gruppen in den USA.

Der Roman hat einen Umfang von 303 Seiten. Daher kann kaum erwartet werden, dass alle Schülerinnen und Schüler ihn vor der Besprechung ganz lesen. Da er in drei Teile geteilt ist, sollte man den Schülerinnen und Schülern jeweils ca. 2 – 3 Wochen Lesezeit pro Teil einräumen, wobei die Interpretation des gesamten Werkes nach 2 Wochen Vorlaufzeit nicht mehr als 8 Schulwochen einnehmen sollte. Darüber hinaus werden *while-reading*-Aufgaben für alle Kapitel gegeben, wenn diese detailliert besprochen werden sollen.
Es sind verschiedene Ausgaben des Romans auf dem Markt. Die Seitenangaben in diesem Unterrichtsmodell beziehen sich auf die Textausgabe des Schöningh Verlags aus der Reihe Einfach Englisch (ISBN 978-3-14-041282-7). Außerdem gibt es ein Audiobook: T. C. Boyle, *The Tortilla Curtain*. Read by the author. Blackstone Audio, Inc., 2006.
Da bei den *while-reading*-Aufgaben Hörverstehensaufgaben berücksichtigt werden, empfiehlt es sich, das Audiobook auch anzuschaffen. Auf Deutsch ist das Buch unter dem Titel *América* erschienen (übersetzt von Werner Richter).

Konzeption des Unterrichtsmodells

Der Roman *The Tortilla Curtain* hat längst seinen Platz im Oberstufenunterricht deutscher Schulen gefunden. Boyle zwingt die Leserschaft, sich mit dem Problem illegaler Einwanderung und Minderheiten auseinander zu setzen, ohne einseitig auf Mitleid für die *minorities* abzuzielen. Durch Delaneys schwankende Haltung ist man aufgefordert, darüber nachzudenken, wie man selbst an seiner Stelle reagieren würde. Diese Auseinandersetzung führt zu Überlegungen, wie in Deutschland mit Minderheiten und gerade in der heutigen Situation (2015) mit Flüchtlingen umgegangen wird, und somit ist der Bezug zu den Lebensumständen der Schülerinnen und Schüler gegeben.

Das vorliegende Unterrichtsmodell will die verschiedenen Aspekte der illegalen Einwanderung aus den im Roman vorgestellten Perspektiven vertiefen. Es bietet sowohl textanalytische Interpretationen als auch kreative und handlungsorientierte Aufgaben. Zu jedem Kapitel gibt es *while-reading*-Aufgaben, die unterschiedlich aufgebaut sind und u. a. eine Hörverstehensaufgabe beinhalten. Weiterhin wird den im neuen Kernlehrplan Englisch (NRW) geforderten Kompetenzbereichen der Sprachmittlung, dem Hörverstehen und dem Sehverstehen Rechnung getragen.

Die Dreiteilung des Romans legt es nahe, den Schülerinnen und Schülern nicht alle 303 Seiten auf einmal als Leseaufgabe zu stellen, sondern die Lesearbeit in drei Teile aufzuteilen. Die Unglücksfälle, die die Protagonisten heimsuchen, werden von Kapitel zu Kapitel verheerender, Delaneys Haltung wird immer radikaler, Cándido und América werden immer verzweifelter.

Der Schwerpunkt der Interpretation liegt auf der Betrachtung von Delaneys Entwicklung und der Frage, wie jemand, der sich selbst als Liberaler bezeichnet, innerhalb weniger Monate zum Reaktionär wird. Daneben wird untersucht, wie die Verzweiflung und der Glaube an den *American Dream* Cándido und América dazu treiben, unter menschenunwürdigen Verhältnissen monatelang unter freiem Himmel zu kampieren.

Die *Components* folgen dem Verlauf des Romans und sollten daher nicht in ihrer Reihenfolge umgestellt werden. Eine Ausnahme bildet *Component 5*, in welchem Zusatzmaterial und Zusatztexte angeboten werden, die man im Verlaufe der Besprechung des Romans jederzeit einsetzen kann. Innerhalb der *Components* werden unterschiedliche Schwerpunkte gesetzt, Aufgabenstellungen und Arbeitsformen variieren. So gibt es z. B. Expertenpuzzles, *Think-Pair-Share*-Vorgehensweise, *hot-seat-procedure* und Diskussionen innerhalb der Lerngruppe. *Mind map*-Arbeit, Wortfeldarbeit, stilistische Analyse und Interpretation von Statistiken werden ebenso berücksichtigt wie kreative Aufgaben.

Zu den angesprochenen Problemstellungen werden Arbeitsblätter und Tafelbilder bereitgestellt, so dass das Modell direkt in den Unterricht einbezogen werden kann. Je nach Bedarf können einzelne Punkte ausgelassen, erweitert oder in Klausuren verwendet werden. Die Bearbeitung eines *Components* erfordert mehrere Unterrichtsstunden, Piktogramme am Rand erleichtern eine schnelle Orientierung über Leitfragen, Sozial- und Arbeitsformen sowie kreative Ansätze. Aufgaben, die sich zur häuslichen Bearbeitung oder für eine Internetrecherche anbieten, sind besonders gekennzeichnet.

Man kann als begleitende Aufgabe einzelne Schülerinnen und Schüler auffordern, pro Kapitel eine kurze Zusammenfassung zu schreiben, die dann in der Klasse zur Orientierung aller in der richtigen Reihenfolge an der Wand aufgehängt werden. Außerdem bietet es sich an, jeweils einer Schülerin/einem Schüler die Aufgabe zu stellen, 10 – 15 wichtige Vokabeln aus je einem Kapitel herauszusuchen, die dann als Lernvokabular oder als Hilfen dem gesamten Kurs zur Verfügung gestellt werden können. Hilfreich in diesem Zusammenhang ist die ebenfalls vom Schöningh-Verlag veröffentlichte annotierte Textausgabe des Romans, die eine Vielzahl von Erklärungen und auch Hinweise zum Lernvokabular liefert.

Die Einstiegsseite des Unterrichtsmodells sollte auf Folie kopiert werden und dient dazu, einen motivierenden Einstieg in den Roman zu bieten. Dies sollte auch erfolgen, wenn die Thematik dem Kurs bereits über Sachtexte vorgestellt wurde.

In ***Component 1***, bezogen auf *part one*, werden nach dem Einstieg in das Thema *migration* anhand einer Collage und/oder der Entwicklung eines Wortfeldes die Protagonisten mit ihren unterschiedlichen Lebensumständen und Einstellungen untersucht. Der Schwerpunkt liegt dabei auf Delaneys Grundhaltung gegenüber der der anderen Weißen in seinem Lebensumfeld und der von América und Cándido gegenüber der von José Navidad. An Aufgaben finden sich u. a. Wortfeldarbeit, die Interpretation von Statistiken, die schauspielerische Umsetzung einer Szene sowie die Analyse des *point of view*, der eine besondere Bedeutung zukommt, da die Erzählperspektive in *The Tortilla Curtain* ständig wechselt und den Leser beeinflusst.
Gleich zu Beginn der Arbeit mit dem Roman sollten die Schülerinnen und Schüler angeregt werden, eine Wandzeitung (Romancollage) im Kursraum anzulegen, die im Verlauf der Unterrichtsreihe mit Arbeitsergebnissen, Bildern, Zusatzinformationen etc. bestückt wird.

Component 2, ebenfalls bezogen auf *part one*, beschäftigt sich schwerpunktmäßig mit den Symbolen, die T.C. Boyle in seinem Roman verwendet. Entscheidend sind in diesem Zusammenhang die *telling names* sowie die Vergleiche, die zwischen den Kojoten und Mexikanern gezogen werden. Ein weiterer Punkt der Analyse ist das *foreshadowing* sowie die Gegenüberstellung der Träume und Lebenswirklichkeit des mexikanischen Paares. Durch die kreative Aufgabe, einen inneren Monolog für América zu schreiben, tauchen die Schüler tief in die Gedanken- und Gefühlswelt dieser Romanfigur ein.

Component 3 bezieht sich auf *part two* und legt einen Schwerpunkt auf die Stilanalyse von Textausschnitten. Die Schülerinnen und Schüler lernen wichtige Stilmittel kennen, suchen in Gruppenarbeit Beispiele aus dem Text und erläutern ihren Gebrauch. Dabei werden die Berührungspunkte, die zwischen Weißen und Mexikanern bestehen, genauer untersucht. Die Interpretation der Symbole, die in *Component 2* vorgestellt wurden, wird wieder aufgenommen. Als *while-reading* Aufgaben sollten in Vorbereitung auf die Arbeit an diesem *Component* beispielsweise Fragen zum Text beantwortet, Statements berichtigt, eine *scrambled summary* sortiert oder Vokabelarbeit geleistet werden. In einer *Hot Seat*-Übung beschäftigt sich der Kurs mit den beiden weiblichen Protagonisten des Romans, Kyra und América.

Component 4, bezogen auf *part one, two and three*, untersucht Delaneys Entwicklung zum Radikalen im Verlauf des gesamten Romans, der eine Waffe in die Hand nimmt, um die Illegalen zu vertreiben. Als Abschluss der Charakterisierung Delaneys versetzen sich die Schülerinnen und Schüler in einer *hot-seat-procedure* in Delaneys Position, wodurch sie angehalten werden, über seine Person gründlich zu reflektieren. Die Auseinandersetzung mit der Symbolik der beiden ersten Teile wird weiterverfolgt. Weiterhin werden wichtige Aussagen aus *Proposition 187* (Kalifornien: 1994) vorgestellt und es wird die nachfolgende politische Entwicklung hinsichtlich illegaler Einwanderung in den USA beleuchtet (***Copy 31*** und ***Copy 32***), was in der Bearbeitung u. a. in einer *timeline* dargestellt wird.

Component 5 bietet eine ganze Reihe von Zusatzmaterialien an, die im Anschluss an die Besprechung des Romans oder während der Lektüre als Hintergrundinformation angeboten werden können. Zunächst dienen die *Touch, turn, talk* – Übung (***Copy 35***) sowie die Aufforderung, über die Reaktionen zu reflektieren, die die einzelnen Figuren im Leser hervorrufen (***Copy 36***) der inhaltlichen Rekapitulation des Gelesenen. ***Copy 37*** präsentiert eine Postkarte, über die die Schüler in Form eines *two/three minute talk* noch einmal direkt Bezüge zu Inhalt und Themen des Romans herstellen können.

Anschließend findet sich eine Hörverstehensaufgabe (***Copy 38***), die sich auf einen *podcast* bezieht, der den Themenbereich *illegal immigration* einschließt. Danach bietet der *Component* Cartoons und eine Anleitung, wie man sie analysiert (***Copies 39*** und ***40***), drei Dokumentationen und Filme über die Thematik der illegalen Einwanderung in den USA, die auf Youtube zu sehen sind und zur emotionalen Auseinandersetzung mit dem Thema auffordern. Des Weiteren wird eine Rede des hispanischen Bürgermeisters von San Antonio zum Thema *The American Dream* angeboten (***Copy 41***), die auch über das Hör- oder Hörsehverstehen erschlossen wird. Der bilinguale Song *Frijolereo* der mexikanischen Gruppe Molotov kritisiert die schlechten Beziehungen zwischen Mexikanern und US-Amerikanern im Grenzgebiet und bietet neben dem Üben des Hörverstehens auch die Möglichkeit zur Mediation (Deutsch, Englisch, Spanisch), ***Copies 43, 44***. Eine Mediationsaufgabe (***Copy 45***) schließt sich an, bei der die Schülerinnen und Schüler einen deutschen Text lesen und herausarbeiten, was er über die Situation junger illegaler Immigranten, die als Kind mit ihren Eltern in die USA eingereist sind, aussagt. ***Copy 46*** bietet eine Auswahl an Blogeinträgen, die unterschiedliche Reaktionen auf den Roman abbilden. Die Aufgabe besteht einerseits darin, die Meinung der Blogger zu erkennen als auch im Anschluss daran, selbst einen solchen Blog als eigene Kritik zu verfassen.

Weiterführende Materialien

T. C. Boyle

www.tcboyle.com
www.tcboyle.net

Onlineartikel und Internetseiten

- zu ***The Tortilla Curtain***
  www.gradesaver.com/the-tortilla-curtain/
  http://home.arcor.de/tortillacurtain/
  https://tcboyletortillacurtain.wordpress.com/weblinks/book-reviews/
  http://www.bookrags.com/studyguide-the-tortilla-curtain/#gsc.tab=0
  http://www.swisseduc.ch/english/readinglist/boyle_tc/tortilla/background.html
  http://www.weberberg.de/skool//tortilla-curtain.html
  http://wikis.zum.de/zum/The_Tortilla_Curtain
  http://partners.nytimes.com/books/98/02/08/home/boyle-tortilla.html
- zu ***Hispanics in the USA***
  http://www.census.gov/newsroom/facts-for-features/2014/cb14–ff22.html
  http://www.infoplease.com/spot/hhmcensus1.html
  http://www.pewhispanic.org/2013/08/29/mapping-the-latino-population-by-state-county-and-city/
  www.nclr.org/

Filme

- *A Day Without a Mexican*. Sergio Arau. USA/Mexiko 2004
- *Bread and Roses*. Ken Loach. United Kingdom, Germany, Spain 2000
- *Cesar Chavez*. Diego Luna. USA 2014
- *Crash*. Paul Haggis. USA 2006
- *Crossing Over*. Wayne Kramer. USA 2008
- *Lake Los Angeles*. Mike Ott. USA 2014
- *La Jaula de Oro*. Diego Quemada- Díez. USA 2013
- *Mexico-USA: The Big Crossing*. Colette Ouanounou. BRD 2003
- *Paraiso Travel*. Simon Brand. Colombia 2008
- *Real Women have Curves*. Patricia Cardoso. USA 2002

- *Spanglish*. James L. Brooks. USA 2004
- *The Gran Torino*. Clint Eastwood. USA 2008

Romane

- Alvarez, Julia: *How the Garcia Girls Lost Their Accents. 1991*
- Alvarez, Julia: *Return to Sender. 2010*
- Castillo, Ana: *The Mixquiahuala Letters.* New York: Doubleday 1986
- Cisneros, Sandra: *The House on Mango Street.* 1984
- Cisneros, Sandra: *Caramelo.* 2002
- Jaramillo, Ann: *La Línea. Klett* 2008
- Junot Diaz, *The Brief Wondrous Life of Oscar Wao,* Riverhead Books New York, 2007
- Rodriguez, Luis J.: *Always Running. La Vida Loca: Gang Days in L.A.* Touchstone 2005
- Vasquez, Richard: *Chicano.* 1970

Short Stories

- Bradbury, R.: *I See You Never.* In: Tepe, Th. (Hrsg.): *Twenty-one New Short Shorts*. Stuttgart: Klett 1995, pp. 94 – 99
- Fondation, L.: *Deportation* at Breakfast. In: Tepe, Th. (Hrsg.): *Twenty-one New Short Shorts*. Stuttgart: Klett 1995, pp. 30 – 32
- Cisneros, S.: *Geraldo No Last Name*. In: *The Before Columbus Fiction Anthology*. Ed. By Ishmael Reed, Kathryn Trueblood and Shawn Wong. New York, London 1992, pp. 511f.

Textsammlungen

- Augenbraum, Harold, Stavans, Ilan (eds.): *Growing up Latino. Memoirs and Stories*. Boston, New York: Houghton Mifflin Company 1993
- Diaz, Rolando J.: *Tales from the Tortilla Curtain and other stories*. Denver: Outskirts Press 2008
- Miller, Tom (ed.): *Writing on the edge. A Borderlands Reader*, The University of Arizona Press 2003

Songs

- Body Count: *Born Dead*. Album: Born Dead. 1994
- Guthrie, Woody (lyrics): *Deportee. (Plane Wreck at Los Gatos).* The song has been covered by many artists, e.g. Joan Baez (1971), Bob Dylan (1976), Dolly Parton (1980), Bruce Springsteen (2000)
- Lila Downs: *La Línea*. Album: Border. Narada Productions 2001.
- Molotov: *Frijolero*. Album: *Dance and Dense Denso*. 2001
- Springsteen, Bruce:
  - *Across the Border*. Album: *The Ghost of Tom Joad*. 1995
  - *Balboa Park*. Album: *The Ghost of Tom Joad*. 1995
  - *Sinaloa Cowboys*. Album: *The Ghost of Tom Joad*. 1995
  - *The Line*. Album: *The Ghost of Tom Joad*. 1995

Poems

- Carlson, Lori M. (ed.): *Cool Salsa: Bilingual poems on growing up Latino in the United States*. New York: Henry Holt & Company: 13th ed. 1994
- Garza Jonson, Erika; Saldana Jr., Rene: *Juventud! Growing up on the Border: Stories and poems*. UAO Publishing 2013
- Miller, Tom (ed.): *Writing on the Edge: a Borderland Reader*. Tucson: The University of Arizona Press 20003
- Oliva, R.: *The Immigrant Experience*. In: Chicano Voices, ed. By Carlota Coridas de Burger. Boston, New York: Houghton Mifflin, pp. 80f.
- Piñero, Miguel: *There is Nothing New In New York*. In: Schunk, Ferdinand (Hrsg.): New York Poems. Stuttgart: Reclam 1991
- Soto, G.: *Mexicans Begin Jogging*. In: Los Angeles. Super City in the Golden State. Compied and edited by Hanspeter Dörfel. München: Langenscheidt-Longman 1996, p. 21
- Stawvan, Llan: *Wachale!: Poetry and Prose about Growing Up Latino in America*. Cricket Books/Mercato 2001

Klausuren

Klausur 1 genügt den neuen Vorgaben, die ab dem Schuljahr 2014/15 für die Sek II in NRW gelten, gemäß derer eine Klausur als reine Textanalyse geschrieben werden kann. Diese Klausur kann im Laufe der Lektüre des Romans gestellt werden, allerdings erst, nachdem die ersten beiden Teile des Romans vollständig und die Kapitel III.1 oder III.2 gelesen wurden. Ebenso sollten die ersten beiden Teile im Unterricht weitgehend bearbeitet worden sein. Es empfiehlt sich, den Schülerinnen und Schülern eine Kopie der Textstelle zur Verfügung zu stellen, wobei sie gleichzeitig mit ihrer Lektüre arbeiten können. Die Kopie dient der Möglichkeit, Passagen großzügig zu unterstreichen bzw. herauszuheben. Die drittletzte Aufgabe in *Component 4* sollte noch nicht bearbeitet worden sein, da sie sich auf die gleiche Textstelle bezieht. Aufgabe 3 ist eine Alternativaufgabe, d.h. die Schülerinnen und Schüler können eine der beiden Aufgaben auswählen. Man kann natürlich auch nur einen der beiden Vorschläge im Aufgabenapparat verwenden. Die Klausur erscheint eher für einen Grundkurs geeignet.

Klausur 2 ist ebenfalls nach den neuen Vorgaben, die ab dem Schuljahr 2014/15 für die Sek II in NRW gelten, konzipiert. Im ersten Teil der Klausur müssen die Schülerinnen und Schüler eine Rede von Präsident Obama analysieren, in der er das Problem der illegalen Einwanderung in die USA und seine Maßnahmen dagegen darlegt. Außerdem macht er den bereits lange illegal im Land lebenden Einwanderern ein Angebot, sich zu offenbaren und Pässe zu beantragen. Im zweiten Teil der Klausur muss ein Artikel aus der Berliner Zeitung, der beschreibt, welche Probleme illegale Einwanderer in Deutschland haben, verstanden und die Hauptaspekte müssen auf Englisch für einen fiktiven Freund zusammengefasst werden (*mediation*). Es ist für die Bearbeitung der Klausur nicht zwingend notwendig, dass der Roman komplett bearbeitet worden ist. Aufgrund der Textmenge empfiehlt sich die Klausur eher für einen Leistungskurs.

T. C. Boyle: *The Tortilla Curtain* (excerpts)

p. 246, l. 4 to l. 38
p. 248, l. 4 to l. 27
p. 248, l. 34 to l. 41

Assignments

1. In the first chapter of the book Delaney is introduced as a liberal humanist. In this excerpt he behaves completely differently. Find passages in which his racist behaviour becomes obvious. The crowd which has gathered at the top of Topanga Canyon consists of affluent Anglo-American people. Describe their behaviour when confronted with the two Mexicans and give reasons for Delaney's change and the behaviour of the crowd. (*Comprehension*)

2. José Navidad is one of the two Mexicans walking up the road. Explain his behaviour towards the Anglo-Americans in this excerpt. To what extent is he different from Cándido and América, the other two Mexicans that play an important role in the book? Analyze their differences using the whole novel as a basis.(*Analysis*)

3. a) Imagine you are the Hispanic cop who arrested the two Mexicans. The following day you meet a friend to whom you describe the entire incident with the two Mexicans and the Anglo-American crowd. (*Re-creation of text*)

OR

b) Discuss the introduction of strict measures such as Proposition 187 in some Southern states to discourage illegal immigration considering this statement taken from President Obama's Immigration Address at American University (July 1, 2015):

"The result is an estimated 11 million undocumented immigrants in the United States. The overwhelming majority of these men and women are simply seeking a better life for themselves and their children. Many settle in low-wage sectors of the economy; they work hard, they save, they stay out of trouble. But because they live in the shadows, they're vulnerable to unscrupulous businesses who pay them less than the minimum wage or violate worker safety rules – thereby putting companies who follow those rules, and Americans who rightly demand the minimum wage or overtime, at an unfair [dis] advantage."
(*Evaluation*)

Erwartungshorizont zu Klausur 1

Zu 1: Delaney is full of hatred when he sees the two Latinos. He tells the police a lie by claiming that he saw José in the canyon where the fire started. When the Mexican spits at him, Delaney attacks him without any restraint. He does not convey any sense of remorse or guilt. Several reasons for this change can be mentioned: an accumulation of unfortunate events related to Mexicans such as Delaney's car hitting Cándido/the theft of his car/Kyra's fear of encountering the Latinos at the Da Ros place and the argument about the wall between Delaney and Kyra/Delaney's consumption of alcohol/the Arroyo Blanco inhabitants turning into a mob under the influence of alcohol and rage/the raging fire/the deep-rooted fear of losing their possessions.
The crowd turns into an uninhibited mob for several reasons: people are under the influence of alcohol/deep-rooted fear of the raging fire/extreme anxiety about their belongings and houses/their subliminal prejudices against Latinos have always been there and are fully released now/they obviously have a psychological need to find a scapegoat, and the two Mexicans suitably meet this need.

Zu 2: José shows a behaviour full of spite and contempt for Anglos. When encountering the crowd he does not display any haste or agitation, but coolness and impassiveness. He wants to show them that he is not interested in their concerns. When he feels Delaney's hateful look resting on him, he is not submissive or intimidated, on the contrary, he becomes offensive and spits at him. His hate results in the threatening phrase "I kill you, motherfucker!" (p. 248, ll. 19f.).
América and Cándido are extremely submissive towards all Anglo-Americans and do not revolt against their predicament. They are nourished by their dream of a better life (apartment, garden, TV, etc) which makes them bear even the most terrible circumstances. They take any kind of work for little money: América cleaning the buddhas with a toxic detergent/Cándido is pushed away like a dog in the parking lot of the supermarket without showing any resistance (pp. 95f.)/América lets her employer grab at her without complaining (p. 89). In contrast to them José displays constant aggressiveness and suspicion. His underprivileged situation has fed his hate towards all Anglos. He acts violently when he is refused at the labour exchange (p. 76)/when encountering Delaney in the canyon (p. 105) und Kyra on the Da Ros property (pp. 144f.) he puts on an indifferent and even mocking manner imposing some kind of menace/he is not even loyal to his own countrymen, interfering with América and finally raping her (pp. 76f./pp. 125f.).

Zu 3:

a) The pupils should try to identify with the Hispanic cop in an authentic manner. They should therefore comment on his feelings about having to arrest two Hispanics and about the reaction of the angry mob. They should also present a plausible and convincing point of view of his role as a Hispanic cop in a police force having to defend white Anglos' rights and pursue illegal Mexican immigrants. This might create an inner conflict in him.

b) Students can take a strict view on illegal immigration thereby agreeing with harsh measures such as the introduction of Proposition 187 offering the following arguments, for example:

- illegal immigrants get low wages and are not provided for as to safety rules which puts companies that only employ "legal workers" at a disadvantage because they have to pay taxes due to paying higher wages and the meeting of security measures
- illegal aliens cost the taxpayer billions of dollars a year
- illegal aliens receive taxpayer-subsidized education including college
- classrooms are overcrowded with illegal children
- illegal aliens get free pre-natal care
- the flow of immigrants has to be stopped because of the financial burden for the country

Students can take a tolerant view on illegal immigration not agreeing with harsh measures such as the introduction of Proposition 187 offering the following arguments, for example:

- the overwhelming majority of Hispanics are seeking a better life in the US due to disastrous conditions in their native countries so they should be given a chance to assimilate to the US society
- Proposition 187 does not keep employers from hiring illegal immigrants, that is why it would be better to naturalize more illegal aliens so they can be officially employed
- the fruit and vegetable picking sector and the restaurant sector in various states would break down if there were no more illegal workers
- if a law like Proposition 187 was introduced, the citizenship of an enormous number of kids in schools would have to be verified and the result would be that lots of kids would be kicked out onto the streets which would put an additional burden on the state
- the health of all Californians would be put at risk if doctors and nurses were forbidden to give immunizations or basic medical care to illegal aliens.

The written comment should start with a plausible introduction of the issue, then the arguments of the position the student has taken should be mentioned. In the same way, some counter-arguments should be given that then are refuted. At the end, the student should present a convincing conclusion.

Part One

Remarks by the President in Address to the Nation on Immigration, Nov. 20, 2014

My fellow Americans, tonight, I'd like to talk with you about immigration.

For more than 200 years, our tradition of welcoming immigrants from around the world has given us a tremendous advantage over other nations. It's kept us youthful, dynamic, and entrepreneurial. It has shaped our character as a people with limitless possibilities – people not trapped by our past, but able to remake ourselves as we choose.

But today, our immigration system is broken – and everybody knows it.

Families who enter our country the right way and play by the rules watch others flout the rules. Business owners who offer their workers good wages and benefits see the competition exploit undocumented immigrants by paying them far less. All of us take offense to anyone who reaps the rewards of living in America without taking on the responsibilities of living in America. And undocumented immigrants who desperately want to embrace those responsibilities see little option but to remain in the shadows, or risk their families being torn apart.

to flout to show that you have no respect

to reap to harvest

It's been this way for decades. And for decades, we haven't done much about it.

When I took office, I committed to fixing this broken immigration system. And I began by doing what I could to secure our borders. Today, we have more agents and technology deployed to secure our southern border than at any time in our history. And over the past six years, illegal border crossings have been cut by more than half. Although this summer, there was a brief spike in unaccompanied children being apprehended at our border, the number of such children is now actually lower than it's been in nearly two years. Overall, the number of people trying to cross our border illegally is at its lowest level since the 1970s. Those are the facts. [...]

spike sudden large increase

The fact is, millions of immigrants in every state, of every race and nationality still live here illegally. And let's be honest – tracking down, rounding up, and deporting millions of people isn't realistic. Anyone who suggests otherwise isn't being straight with you. It's also not who we are as Americans. After all, most of these immigrants have been here a long time. They work hard, often in tough, low-paying jobs. They support their families. They worship at our churches. Many of their kids are American-born or spent most of their lives here, and their hopes, dreams, and patriotism are just like ours. [...]

to round up to gather

to be straight with to be honest with

We expect people who live in this country to play by the rules. We expect that those who cut the line will not be unfairly rewarded. So we're going to offer the following deal: If you've been in America for more than five years; if you have children who are American citizens or legal residents; if you register, pass a criminal background check, and you're willing to pay your fair share of taxes – you'll be able to apply to stay in this country temporarily without fear of deportation. You can come out of the shadows and get right with the law.

to cut the line to skip those before you in a line

(506 words)

Remarks by the President in Address to the Nation on Immigration, November 20, 2014; online: https://www.whitehouse.gov/the-press-office/2014/11/20/remarks-president-address-nation-immigration [29.01.2016]

Assignments

1. Summarize what problems Obama names with regard to illegal immigration and which measures he suggests to fight the problem.
2. Analyse the way the President convinces the audience of his ideas taking into consideration structure and use of language.

3. You have a choice:

a) Comment on Obama's statement "tracking down, rounding up, and deporting millions of people isn't realistic [...] It's also not who we are as Americans." (ll. 24 – 36). Refer to the text at hand and what you have discussed in class.

OR

b) Cándido and América have survived the flood. They are taken into a hospital where they watch Obama's speech on TV. Write their dialogue.

Part Two

Ohne Ärzte, ohne Lehrer, ohne Richter

In ihrem Leben darf nichts schief gehen. Sie können es sich nicht leisten, krank zu werden oder sich zu verletzen, denn zum Arzt trauen sie sich nicht. Sie müssen darauf hoffen, dass ihr Arbeitgeber ihnen den vereinbarten Lohn zahlt, denn einklagen können sie ihn nicht. Wenn sie Glück haben, geraten sie an einen anständigen Vermieter, denn gegen Mietwucher sind sie hilflos. Ihre Kinder kommen heimlich auf die Welt, Geburtsurkunden gibt es für sie nicht. Kindergarten, Schule? Besser nicht, zu groß ist die Gefahr, in das Blickfeld der Ausländerbehörde zu geraten und ausgewiesen zu werden. Hunderttausende, vielleicht sogar eine Million solcher Menschen, leben in Deutschland, Wirtschaftsflüchtlinge, die hier ausdrücklich nicht erwünscht sind. Sie stammen aus Russland, Iran, Afghanistan, Ex-Jugoslawien oder Vietnam und sind in der Hoffnung auf ein besseres Leben nach Deutschland gekommen. Anspruch auf politisches Asyl haben sie nicht, nun schlagen sie sich durch als Putzhilfen, Altenpfleger, Bauarbeiter oder Erntehelfer. Ihr steter Begleiter ist die Angst, den Behörden aufzufallen. Anders als andere reiche Staaten hat Deutschland Stichtags-Regelungen für ihre Legalisierung stets abgelehnt, aus Angst, noch mehr Migranten anzuziehen. Zwar gelten auch für sie Grundrechte wie das auf Entlohnung für geleistete Arbeit oder ärztliche Versorgung, aber sie werden kaum je geltend gemacht. Denn öffentliche Einrichtungen wie Schulen, Gerichte oder Krankenhäuser sind verpflichtet, illegale Ausländer an die Ausländerbehörde zu melden. Kirchen und Wohlfahrtsverbände fordern schon lange, diese Vorschriften zu lockern. [...] Doch größere Verbesserungen wird es wohl nicht geben. Denn zuständig ist das Innenministerium, und das will vor allem eines: den Zuzug weiterer Migranten stoppen. Die Meldepflichten sollen daher sogar ausgeweitet werden. Künftig sollen nicht nur die Schulleiter verpflichtet sein, Familien ohne Papiere bei der Anmeldung ihrer Kinder anzuzeigen. Auch die Lehrer, wenn sie zufällig Kenntnis vom Status ihrer Schüler erhalten, müssen dann die Ausländerbehörde informieren. Nur in einem Punkt zeigt sich das Ministerium kompromissbereit: Ärzten, die Illegale behandeln, wird ausdrücklich attestiert, dass sie sich damit nicht strafbar machen.

Bettina Vestring: Ohne Ärzte, ohne Lehrer, ohne Richter, Berliner Zeitung, 22.12.2007; online: http://www.berliner-zeitung.de/archiv/eine-million-illegaler-einwanderer-leben-in-deutschland--fuer-die-die-politik-nichts-tun-will-ohne-aerzte--ohne-lehrer--ohne-richter,10810590,10527326.html [29.01.2016]

Assignments

Your friend John in California has just read *The Tortilla Curtain* in class and must now work on a project about the situation of illegal immigrants in European countries. He must collect information about where illegals come from, what jobs they can get in Germany and what rights they have. He has asked you to help him.
You have read the article in the *Berliner Zeitung* and so you can give him some information about this topic. Write the part of your email in which you answer his question.

Erwartungshorizont zu Klausur 2

Zu 1: Problems of illegal immigration:

- our immigration system is broken (l. 6)
- illegals flout the rules and so honest immigrants are deprived of their chances (ll. 7/8)
- American business owners employ illegal workers for pitiful wages such driving honest businesses out (l. 9)
- illegal immigrants are forced to remain anonymous (l. 12)

Measures to fight the problem:

- secure the borders (l. 16) → illegal border crossings have been halfed (l. 18)
- millions of immigrants live in America illegally (ll. 23/24)
- Obama offers all illegal immigrants a deal – they can stay legally if they have lived in America for more than 5 years, are not criminal and are willing to pay taxes (ll. 31 – 34)

Zu 2: Structure:

- Speech starts with address "fellow Americans" and a sentence that makes the audience feel personally addressed: "I'd like to talk with you" (l. 1).
- Short reflection about the history of America as a country which has always attracted a large number of immigrants (ll. 2 – 5).
- Obama lists the problems that illegal immigrants cause – they deprive legal immigrants of their chances, corrupt businesses by working for less money than honest bosses pay (ll. 8 – 11).
- The President lists the successes he has had since he became president – the border controls have been enforced and so the number of illegal immigrants has dropped dramatically – it is the lowest since the 1970s (ll. 16 – 22)
- Indirectly Obama refutes the opposition's suggestions to catch all illegal immigrants and send them back to their home countries. He points out that all these immigrants take part in American life (ll. 24 – 29).
- Obama makes the offer to allow illegal immigrants to stay in the country if they fulfil certain criteria (ll. 30 – 36).

Use of language:

a) Stylistic devices:

- enumeration: "It's kept us youthful, dynamic, and entrepreneurial" (ll. 3/4) → audience feels flattered; "tracking down, rounding up, and deporting" (l. 24) → it is simply impossible to send millions of people away; "their hopes, dreams, and patriotism" (l. 29) →illegal immigrants share the same values as American citizens;
- repetition: "..for decades. And for decades" (l. 14) → Obama stresses for how long America has faced the problem of illegal immigration and that not enough has been done to fight it; "our immigration system is broken" (l. 6) – "this broken immigration system" (l. 15) (also chiasm and metaphor) → the system does not work – it must be fixed; "to play by the rules" (ll. 7 and 30) → Obama emphasizes the fact that only immigrants who respect laws are welcome in the US; "to remain in the shadows" (l. 15) "come out of the shadows" (l. 35) (also metaphor and antithesis) → the metaphor stresses the awful life illegal immigrants lead because they cannot come into the light and participate in everyday activities with other citizens;
- metaphor: "people trapped by our past" (l. 5) → new immigrants start new lives without the burden of past history; "who reaps the rewards of living in America" (l. 10) → people who just want to enjoy America's offers without taking responsibility are not welcome, they harvest without having sown;
- anaphora: "If you've been ... if you have ... if you register ..." (ll. 31 – 34) → the deal is explained, everybody who ticks all these boxes can stay.

b) use of personal pronouns: Obama uses "our" and "I" when talking about his success (ll. 15 ff.) and "we" when he talks about his deal and what all Americans expect of illegal immigrants who want to come clean (ll. 30 ff.). He addresses the illegals directly by using "you" when he makes that offer (ll. 32 ff.).

c) use of adjectives: When talking about the back breaking jobs many illegal immigrants must do to survive he uses "hard, tough, low-paying" (l. 27) to show how bad working conditions in these jobs are.

d) use of statistics: in order to support his statements Obama uses statistics and numbers "over the past six years, illegal border crossings have been cut by more than half" (l. 18), "the lowest level since the 1970s" (l. 22).

Zu 3 a):
Students should comment on the fact that America has always welcomed immigrants from all over the world and give examples from history. They should also explain that the problem of illegal immigration cannot be solved by asking for measures to send every illegal person back to their home countries because that task would be too much for the authorities and would also mean that many employers would lose their cheap labour force and thus would lead to a sharp increase in prices for fruit and vegetables.
There should be a reference to the novel, e. g. the scene when Cándido crosses the highway in a fit of frenzy and indirectly causes the death of two young Mexican men.

b):
Students should make clear that the deal does not apply to Cándido and América since they have neither lived in the US for five years nor have they ever paid taxes. The situation does not change for them and they must come to a conclusion about where to go and what to do.

Possible solutions part two:

- Illegal immigrants come from countries where they cannot find jobs, like Russia, Iran, Afghanistan, former Yugoslavia and Vietnam.
- They find jobs as cleaners, old people's nurses, construction workers and harvest hands.
- They have the right to get paid adequately for their work, but it is difficult for them to get heard when they are cheated. They also have the right to get medical treatment. Their problem is that public institutions must report them when they find out that they live in Germany illegally.

Component 1

When worlds clash

1.1 First encounter and clashes between the two worlds

Der erste *Component* beschäftigt sich mit der Erarbeitung des ersten Teils des Romans (Part one: *Arroyo Blanco*). Dabei werden zwei Hauptaspekte beleuchtet, zum einen die Erstbegegnung der beiden Welten mit der sich dabei ergebenden Problematik der illegalen Einwanderung in die USA und zum anderen die unterschiedlichen Sichtweisen und Haltungen einiger zentraler Figuren zur Einwanderung im Allgemeinen.

Voraussetzung für die erste Stunde ist, dass *Part I* des Romans ganz gelesen wurde, die Kapitel I. 1, I. 3, I. 6 und I. 7 intensiv, die anderen extensiv. Bei der häuslichen Lektüre werden die Schüler durch unterschiedliche *while reading*-Aufgaben (***Copies 6 – 12***) zu jedem Kapitel motiviert und unterstützt. Die Lösungsvorschläge finden sich alle hier.

Solutions while reading assignments Part one

Copy 6

1. Delaney lives 32 Piñon Drive, Arroyo Blanco Estates. (p. 10, ll. 7 f.)
2. He wants to take it to the recycler. (p. 10, ll. 22 f.)
3. He thinks of his car and insurance rate first. (p. 3, ll. 37 f.)
4. The other drivers just pass by indifferently. Nobody stops to help. (p. 11, ll. 26 – 28)
5. Yes, the victim is severely hurt. (p. 13, ll. 32 – 39)
6. Delaney does not speak Spanish; the victim does not speak English. (p. 14, ll. 11 – 28)
7. He asks for money. (p. 15, l. 8)
8. He is an illegal immigrant and fears to get deported. (p. 16, ll. 16 f.)
9. The idea makes him feel outraged. (p. 11, l. 41)
10. Delaney has been living in Los Angeles for nearly two years. (p. 17, l. 26)
11. Delaney tells his car dealer that he hit an animal. (p. 18, l. 35)
12. The headlight has to be fixed. (p. 19, l. 41)

Copy 7

1. Wrong; he had two hard-cooked eggs, half a cup of coffee and a tortilla. (p. 21, ll. 10 f.)
2. Right (p. 21, l. 15; p. 22, ll. 11 – 20)
3. Wrong; she takes the bus to Venice to find a job. (p. 22, l. 37)
4. Right (p. 24, l. 5)
5. Wrong; as a little boy Cándido lived in Tepoztlán, in the South of Mexico. (p. 24, ll. 29 f.)
6. Right (p. 25, ll. 37 – 42)
7. Wrong (p. 25, l. 12)
8. Right (p. 27, l. 1)
9. Right (p. 27, ll. 17 – 20)
10. Wrong (p. 28, l. 43 –p. 29, l. 14)
11. Right (p. 29, l. 28)

Copy 8, I

1. breakfast (p. 33, l. 23 – p. 34, l. 3)
2. coyote (p. 38, l. 44)
3. dogs (p. 39, l. 1)
4. hill (p. 39, ll. 24 ff.)
5. meeting (p. 41, l. 15)
6. gate/fence (p. 42, l. 18)
7. disapproval/warning (p. 45, ll. 19 ff.)
8. son (p. 46, l. 23)
9. accident (p. 47, ll. 3 ff.)

Copy 8, II

1. ... to offer herself at the labour exchange; she needs a job. (p. 48, ll. 1 f.)
2. ... he has no choice; he has to let her go because he is unable to work. (p. 49, ll. 8 – 15)
3. ... his worries about América and his first wife, Resurección. (p. 49, ll. 33 ff.)
4. ... she is an adult and old enough to work. (p. 54, ll. 2 ff.)
5. ... men, staring at América. (p. 54, ll. 19 ff.)
6. ... they check out their camp and finally destroy their fireplace. (p. 59, ll. 8 ff.)
7. ... "beaners" is a swearword for Mexicans. (p. 60, l. 10)

Copy 9

1. p. 61, ll. 1 f., ll. 11 f.
2. p. 62, ll. 27 – 29
3. p. 65, ll. 11 – 13
4. p. 67, ll. 36 f.
5. p. 68, ll. 29 f.
6. p. 69, ll. 27 f.
7. p. 70, l. 24
8. p. 72, l. 5

Copy 10

1. b: p. 75, ll. 1 – 12
2. a: p. 75, ll. 38 ff.
3. a: p. 78, ll. 22 f.
4. c: p. 80, ll. 19 – 22
5. a: p. 82, ll. 29 – 31
6. b: p. 84, ll. 37 f.
7. b: p. 85, ll. 20 ff.
8. a: p. 88, ll. 24 – 28
9. c: p. 89, l. 18

Copy 11

1. He is in a hurry because the dinner he was cooking is almost ready. Kyra is about to get home and Jordan is waiting in the car in the supermarket's parking lot. (p. 90, l. 2; p. 91, l. 12; p. 92, ll. 41 f.)
2. He thinks the gate is important for the residents' safety and claims self-protection and prudence as a justification for the construction of the gate. (p. 92, l. 16)
3. He says it is racist (p. 92, l. 27) and reminds Jack of the fact that the USA is a nation of immigrants. (p. 93, ll. 1 – 3)

4. The United States has to spend a great part of its tax revenues to cover for the crimes committed by immigrants and for the social services they need (p. 93, ll. 14f.), especially for welfare, emergency care and schooling (p. 93, ll. 27f.).
5. No (p. 108, l. 29)
6. He must constantly think of Cándido. (p. 98, l. 38)
7. First he is amazed (p. 101, l. 37), then he feels embarrassed (p. 102, l. 3), and finally he is outraged. (p. 102, ll. 12ff.)
8. He is afraid because he has heard stories of crimes that were committed in the canyon. (p. 103, ll. 13f.)
9. He thinks that the police towed it because he didn't respect the parking rules. (p. 107, ll. 18f.)
10. Cándido comes to his mind. (p. 108, ll. 36f.)

Copy 12: Correct order: 7 – 4 – 10 – 8 – 1 – 6 – 3 – 2 – 5 – 9

Für den Einstieg werden zwei unterschiedliche Verfahren vorgeschlagen. Erstens kann man mit den Schülerinnen und Schülern ein Wortfeld zum Thema *migration* zusammenstellen. Dazu wird zunächst ein *cluster* mit passenden Begriffen in einem Unterrichtsgespräch entwickelt.

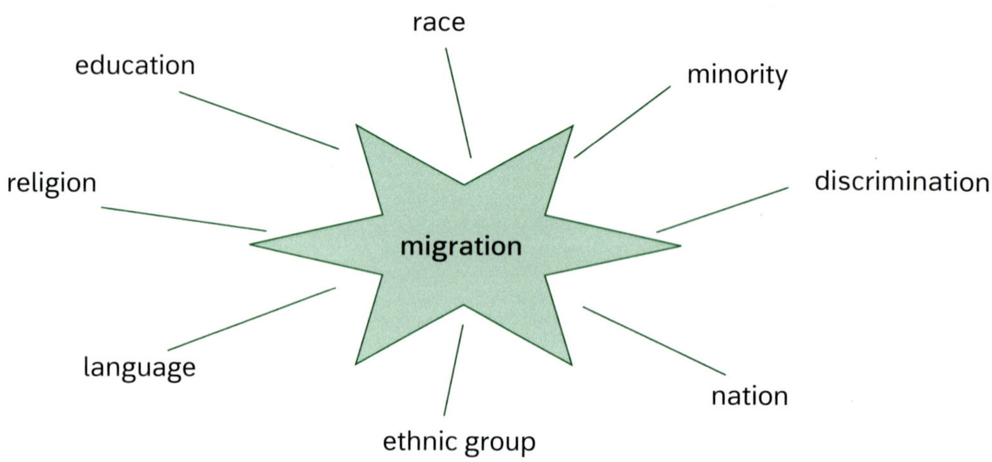

Da sich diese Begriffe relativ logisch und zwingend aus dem Thema ergeben sind sie auf ***Copy 1*** schon vorgeben. In die noch freien Felder können weitere Oberbegriffe von den Schülerinnen und Schülern eingetragen werden. Aus vorangegangenen Unterrichtsreihen und durch die Lektüre von *The Tortilla Curtain* sind den Schülerinnen und Schülern schon viele Wörter und Wendungen zum Thema bekannt, so dass sie in Partner- oder Kleingruppen arbeiten können. Wichtig ist, dass dieses Wortfeld im Laufe der Unterrichtsreihe immer weiter entwickelt wird. Eine Möglichkeit wäre auch, das Wortfeld in Form einer Wandzeitung festzuhalten, die auch durch Bilder oder Zeichnungen ergänzt wird.

Der zweite Vorschlag zum Einstieg konfrontiert die Schülerinnen und Schüler zur Einstimmung auf die Thematik des Romans mit der am Anfang dieses Unterrichtsmodells abgebildeten Collage (auf Folie), die Bilder aus der kalifornisch-mexikanischen Grenzregion zeigt. Als stummer Impuls oder durch folgende Frage angeregt nehmen die Schülerinnen und Schüler spontan Stellung.

> Describe the picture in detail.
> Comment on the function of the fence.
> What does the traffic sign express?

Bei der Besprechung der Collage (*Getting Started*-Seite) werden von den Schülerinnen und Schülern sicherlich Ergebnisse aus vorhergegangenen Unterrichtsreihen oder im Laufe der Lektüre des Romans *The Tortilla Curtain* erworbene Kenntnisse eingebracht werden, z. B. Wissen über die hispanische Immigration in die USA, die Situation an der Grenze, die spezifischen geographischen Gegebenheiten sowie über die politische Diskussion zum Thema.

Folgende Aspekte werden im Unterrichtsgespräch vermutlich genannt werden:

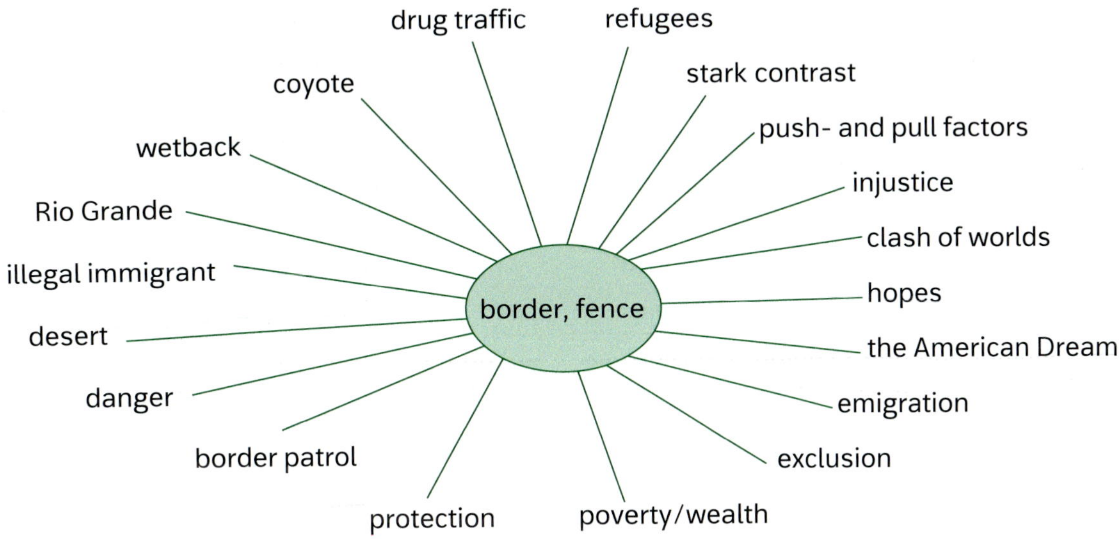

the immigrants' point of view | **the Americans' point of view**

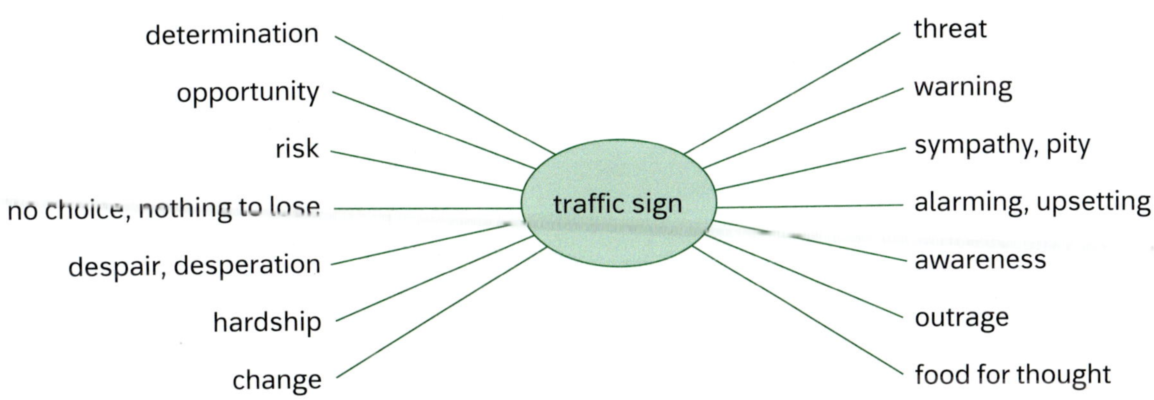

Im Anschluss werden die (schon in Hausarbeit bearbeiteten) *while-reading*-Aufgaben zu *part one* (***Copies 6 – 12***) besprochen, um das grobe inhaltliche Verständnis des Inhalts sicher zu stellen. Dies kann (abwechselnd) in Partner- oder Kleingruppenarbeit oder im Plenum erfolgen. Zu Beginn der intensiven Auseinandersetzung mit Delaney, einer der Hauptfiguren, wird dann der Inhalt des ersten Kapitels von *part one* von einem Schüler kurz mündlich zusammengefasst.

Daraufhin wird die Aufmerksamkeit durch folgende (im *think-pair-share*-Verfahren zu bearbeitende) Aufgabenstellung auf Delaney gelenkt:

- Read chapter I, 1 again and mark the passages that give the reader information on Delaney's behaviour.
- Then get together with a partner, compare your results and draw conclusions about Delaney's attitudes/character traits.
- Present your results in class.

Bei der Besprechung der Ergebnisse kann sich folgendes Tafel-/Folienbild ergeben:

information	evidence	conclusion
Delaney Mossbacher lives with his wife and son in Southern California.	p. 10, pp. 19f.	
He drives a well-kept, expensive car.	p. 10, pp. 18	wealthy, upper middle class
He is described as a liberal humanist.	p. 10	open, tolerant, benevolent, human
He takes bottles to the recycler's and is outraged at the trash he finds in the countryside.	p. 10 p. 16	environmentally friendly, nature lover
After the accident, his first thought is for his car.	p. 10	egoistic, selfish, materialist
He accuses the victim of provoking the accident.	p. 10, p. 13	rejects responsibility
Then he worries about the person he has hit.	p. 10	sympathetic
He looks for the victim, offers help.	p. 10, p. 13	responsible, helpful
He is relieved when he realizes that he has not killed anybody because a dead victim would mean a lot of trouble for him.	p. 14	selfish
He does not call the police (he knows the illegal Mexican will not report the accident to the police or sue him).		feel safe; superior
First he offers to take the Mexican to a doctor, then (on the request of the Mexican) gives him some money instead; he buys him off.	p. 15	feeling of superiority (?) ambivalence
He feels pity for the desperate situation of the Mexican.	pp. 15f.	sympathetic
He is surprised to see so many Mexicans working at the recycler's.	p. 17	ignorant, not aware of the world around him, self-centered
He lies to the car dealer about the cause of the accident.	p. 18	feeling of shame, guilt
He calls the money he gave the Mexican "blood money".	p. 19	self-doubt, pangs of remorse
He tells Kyra that "nobody is hurt."	p. 19	discriminating, inhuman (?) protective of his wife (?)
He tells Kyra that he thinks a compensation of only 20 $ for the badly injured victim is enough because he is Mexican.	p. 20	arrogant, racist, prejudiced

➡ discrepancy between Delaney's liberal humanist ideals and his arrogant, selfish, racist behaviour after the accident
➡ inner conflict

Als Hausaufgabe zur nächsten Stunde nehmen die Schüler in einem kurzen Kommentar Stellung zu Delaneys Verhalten und fertigen eine Zusammenfassung von Teil I, Kapitel 6 an.

Examine Delaney's behaviour after the accident. Write a short comment in an email to your classmates.
Write a summary of part one, chapter 6.

Nachdem ein Schüler die in Hausarbeit gefertigte Zusammenfassung des Inhalts von Teil I, Kapitel 6 vorgetragen hat, konzentriert sich diese Stunde auf die Figur des José Navidad, dessen charakteristische Merkmale herausgearbeitet werden sollen. In arbeitsteiliger Gruppenarbeit trägt Gruppe 1 die Informationen zu seinem äußeren Erscheinungsbild auf Folie zusammen; Gruppe 2 die Informationen zu seinem Verhalten.

José Navidad is another central character among the Mexicans. Describe his characteristic features as presented in part one, chapter 6.
Group 1: Focus on outward appearance.
Group 2: Focus on behaviour.

Es werden sich in etwa folgende Ergebnisse ergeben:

Characteristic features of José Navidad	
outward appearance	behaviour
• tall (p. 75, l. 35) • wears a baseball cap turned backwards (p. 75, l. 36) • light skin (p. 75, l. 37) • hard burnished unblinking eyes the color of calf's liver (p. 75, ll. 39 f.) • jabbing out at the world like two weapons (p. 76, ll. 3 f.) • there is something wrong with his teeth, something rotting inside of him (p. 77, ll. 8 ff.) • wears cheap dentures (p. 77, l. 11)	• curses when refused a job at the labor exchange (p. 76, l. 30) • approaches América in an aggressive and intrusive manner (pp. 76 f.) • shows curiosity towards Cándido, questions him about camping in the canyon (p. 82) • embodies a menace to Cándido (l. 83, ll. 3 f.)
➡ filthy, shabby impression, scary, frightening	➡ threatening not to be trusted

Nachdem José Navidad näher betrachtet wurde, bietet es sich jetzt an, die beiden zentralen mexikanischen Figuren, América und Cándido, in den Blickpunkt zu rücken. Auf der Grundlage von Kapiteln I, 1 und I, 6 kann erst einmal allgemein besprochen werden, dass die Persönlichkeiten des Paares América und Cándido auf der einen Seite und ihres Landsmannes José auf der anderen Seite recht konträr sind. Ebenso differieren ihre Haltungen zu den spezifischen Lebensbedingungen und Herausforderungen nach der Flucht in die USA gewaltig. Hierzu bietet sich ein Gruppenpuzzle an, bei dem sich die Mitglieder jeder Gruppe in einem ersten Schritt auf eine der drei Figuren konzentriert und dann in gemischten Gruppen ihre Ergebnisse austauschen.

Work out the attitudes of América, Cándido and José towards the living and working conditons in the US and the American people they encounter (chapter I, 1 and chapter I, 6).

Abschließend kann sich zur Sicherung der Ergebnisse folgendes Tafel-/Folienbild ergeben:

Attitudes towards their new lives in the USA

América

- accepts any kind of work for little money (p. 78)
- works extremely hard to make a good impression (p. 85)
- lets her employer grab at her without complaining (p. 89)
- stealing is something immoral to her which she only does in an extreme emergency (p. 58)

Cándido

- ready to take any kind of work for little money (p. 75)
- is prepared to work hard to make a good impression (p. 75)
- never complains or shouts at Americans (pp. 13 f./p. 85)
- never tries to take advantage of a situation (pp. 13 f.)

} Both are willing to bear any hardship and suffering in order to stay in the US. They believe in the American Dream.

José

- the submissive position he had to take toward whites has made him evil (pp. 75 f.)
- defiant attitude towards the headman at the labor exchange (p. 76)
- is not willing to wait patiently for his turn (p. 76)
- the talks to Cándido in an intrusive and menacing manner (p. 82 f.)
- the baseball cap turned backwards indicates an obstinate attitude towards the poor circumstances he lives in (p. 75)

} He openly shows his loathing of the miserable situation he finds himself in. He has been disappointed by the United States.

Es bietet sich an, als Hausaufgabe eine kreative Schreibaufgabe zu stellen, bei der die Schüler gehalten sind, sich näher mit der Person der América auseinanderzusetzen, indem sie versuchen, sich unter folgender Aufgabenstellung in ihre Gefühls- und Gedankenwelt hineinzuversetzen:

> Put yourself in América's position and describe in an interior monologue how you reacted to Cándido's accident and the experiences and feelings you had when you found your first job. (chapter I, 1, chapter 1, 6).

Bei der Bearbeitung dieser Aufgabe kommt es darauf an, dass die Schüler die Fakten korrekt wiedergeben und die Gefühle und Stimmungen der Person der América authentisch beschreiben. ***Copy 2*** *„How to write an interior momolugue"* unterstützt die Schüler bei dieser Aufgabe.

Hier finden sich sowohl Informationen zu textuellen Aspekten des Zieltextformates als auch Vokabelhilfen.

Im Anschluss an die Betrachtung der drei Mexikaner erfolgt in der nächsten Stunde eine kurze Einführung bzw. Wiederholung des Komplexes *point of view*. Dazu werden die Informationen zu den drei wichtigsten Erzählperspektiven und die drei Illustrationen von ***Copy 3*** ausgeschnitten und den Schülern (paar- oder kleingruppenweise) in einem Umschlag ausgehändigt. Aufgabe ist nun, die Bilder den entsprechenden Texten zuzuordnen. Alternativ (oder differenzierend) können auch nur die Texte ausgegeben werden und die Schüler fertigen ein Bild zur Illustration an und/oder nur die Bilder werden ausgeteilt und schriftlich erläutert.

Anschließend wird folgende Aufgabenstellung als Hausaufgabe gegeben.

1. Analyse the narrators's point of view in chapter I. 1
2. Tell the story in chapter I. 1 from Cándido's point of view.
3. Explain the effect of the change of point of view on the reader.

Es wird etwa folgendes Ergebnis erwartet:

1. The narrator tells his story through Delaney's eyes. The reader learns everything about Delaney's feelings and emotions, but sees only what Delaney observes about other people. So there is a third-person selective-omniscient author. As the reader you can easily identify with Delaney since his feelings and emotions after the accident are conveyed to you very clearly.

Bei der zweiten Aufgabe kommt es darauf an, dass alle Tatsachen korrekt angesprochen werden und Cándidos eigenes Erleben möglichst authentisch wiedergegeben wird. Eine mögliche Lösung wäre die folgende Schülerarbeit aus einem 12. Jahrgang:

2. I had a really nasty experience. Maybe you think I'm insane, but I don't mind, I need to tell you, really, ... About a month ago I went to the labour exchange, but as usual there was no work for me, you know what I'm talking about. Then I went over to the supermarket to get some nachos and something to drink. I spent my last bucks on these.
   After that, carrying the shopping bag, I made my way back to the camp in the canyon. When I crossed the street and was trying to reach the other side one of those gringo cars faced me, a pile of chrome and metal.
   I couldn't even think of escaping that monstrous mass, then I found myself on the hood, and bounced right into the shrubs. That hit me hard, man! Gave me a beating I'll never forget! When I regained consciousness I stared right into the face of that gringo, you know, one of those pencil-pusher guys.
   He was mumbling something like calling a doctor, but my body felt like I had been run over by a steamroller. There was pain in every limb of my body. How did that guy manage to ram into me!
   Right when I crossed the street that paranoid rushed round the corner, I mean, why didn't he see me? You usually see somebody crossing the street, unless you are blind but I think that guy wasn't blind because otherwise he wouldn't be allowed to drive. I bet he dreamed of his promotion or how he was going to wash and wax his car, those gringos always do! And when he was dreaming, he suddenly heard a loud noise, something like a muffled thump which was me, crushed onto the hood.

The only thing they've got in mind is money, possession, influence, ... pinche pendejos! Do you know what he gave me as a compensation, you know that? He gave me 20 bucks for crippling me!
I mean, what am I supposed to do now? América is pregnant and I need to recover. Does that guy really think that $ 20 are enough to pay for the destruction of the lives of three human beings? I'm so sorry for you gringos, I'd rather be a wreck than be as vile as you.

3. The fact that the author T. C. Boyle presents the accident from two different perspectives emphasizes the stark contrast between Delaney's comfortable white upper-middle class world and the appalling conditions the illegal immigrant has to face.

Um den zweiten Aspekt des ersten *Component* einzuleiten, die Haltung der zentralen Figuren zur Einwanderungsproblematik, ist es sinnvoll, die Schüler mit Hintergrundwissen zu versehen. Die Fakten zur Geschichte der USA als Land der Einwanderer könnten durch ein Schülerkurzreferat zum Thema „Immigration into the US from the end of the 19th century until today" vermittelt werden. Die Informationen zur neueren Einwanderung, speziell der *Hispanics*, erarbeiten die Schüler sich anhand des statistischen Materials auf ***Copy 4*** in arbeitsteiliger Gruppenarbeit (drei Gruppen). Jede Gruppe bearbeitet eine der auf ***Copy 4*** vorgeschlagenen Aufgaben. Anschließend finden sich die Schüler in Dreiergruppen mit jeweils einem Vertreter aus den vorigen Gruppen zusammen und stellen sich gegenseitig ihre Ergebnisse vor. Unterstützung zur Versprachlichung der Auswertung der Statistiken bietet ***Copy 5***.

Form three groups of an equal number of people. Each group works on one of the assignments of *Copy 4* and interprets the given data. After that get together with three students in one group, each one presenting the results of a different assignment.

Beispielhaft ist im Folgenden ein Lösungsvorschlag für Aufgabe 2 ausgearbeitet, die darauf abzielt, die Schüler die Korrelation zwischen fallendem (niedrigen) Bruttoinlandsprodukt in der mexikanischen Wirtschaft und der steigenden Anzahl von Auswanderern bei gleichzeitig sinkender Anzahl von Rückkehrern erkennen zu lassen. Im Zusammenhang mit dem Roman, der 1995 erschien, ist die Information auf *Chart 3* interessant, die für dieses Jahr ein extrem niedriges BIP für Mexiko verzeichnet.

Solution *Copy 4*: Assignment 2

2. Explain the development of the number of people departing from Mexico and returning to Mexico in relation with the development of the gross domestic product (GDP) in Mexico between 2006 and 2007 (Charts 2 and 3).

- Chart 2 is a line graph published by the Mexican National Institute of Statistics and Geography, National Survey of Occupation and Employment, 2006 to 2011 that shows the emigration rate of Mexican residents from 2006 to 2011 in absolute numbers of persons per 1,000 in a dark green line and the return migration rate of Mexican residents in a light green line. It becomes obvious that the light green line falls when the dark green line rises. At a time when a high number of persons leave Mexico (e.g. almost 11,000 in Q2, 2007), a low number of Mexicans return to their country (approximately 3,000 in Q2, 2007).
- Chart 3 is a line graph published by the Economist Intelligence Unit that shows the real gross domestic product (GDP) in Mexico between 1985 and 2009 in percentage figures indicating the change. The graph presents a high

growth of about 5 % for the year 2006 followed by a steep fall that reaches approximately – 7 % in 2008.

- Comparing the information given in charts 2 and 3 of the years 2006 to 2008, you can conclude that a strong decrease in the GDP development (from the highest growth in 2006 to the lowest in 2008) is the reason for a very high number of people emigrating from Mexico (and a very low number of migrants returning to Mexico). The given data allow the conclusion that the dropping GDP means poor living conditions for many Mexicans and thus is responsible for their emigration (push-factor).

1.2 Conflicting points of view on the immigration issue

Der zweite Teil dieses *Components* befasst sich mit den unterschiedlichen Haltungen zur Errichtung eines Zaunes mit bewachtem Eingangstor um Arroyo Blanco herum, die von verschiedenen Bewohnern während einer Versammlung geäußert werden. Zunächst werden die Schülerinnen und Schüler aufgefordert, diese Meinungen aus Kapitel I,3 herauszuarbeiten. Zeitökonomisch kann dies in arbeitsteiliger Gruppenarbeit erfolgen, wobei jede Gruppe sich auf eine Figur (Jim Shirley, the athlete, Jack Cherrystone, Delaney) konzentriert und eine Folie zur Ergebnispräsentation vorbereitet.

Read p. 42, l. 1 – p. 46 l. 14 again. Describe and explain the different opinions on the building of a gate voiced by the residents of Arroyo Blanco during their meeting. Focus on Jim Shirley, the athlete, Jack Cherrystone or Delaney and prepare a transparency to present your findings.

Folgendes Folienbild könnte sich ergeben:

Opinions on the building of the gate voiced during the meeting of the residents

Jim Shirley

- houses broken into after a fixed pattern (p. 43)

➡ emphasis on the security of the residents

athlete

- prefers an open community without fences, not only for privileged people (p. 44)

➡ no elitist behaviour or discrimination of any group

Jack Cherrystone

- basically wants to live humanist ideals but as the world is in such an immoral state he thinks it is naive to do so
- therefore he favors the gate as something vital (p. 44)

➡ disillusion about the outside world: secluded community important to live freely

Delaney

- tries to voice his disapproval of the residents' tendency to feed coyotes and other wild animals (pp. 44 f.)

➡ nature lover's point of view

Nach dieser inhaltlichen Vorbereitung ist es eine reizvolle vertiefende Aufgabe, diese Szene von den Schülern nachspielen zu lassen, da es sich um eine hitzige Diskussion zu einem zentralen Thema handelt. T.C. Boyle beschreibt die Stimmung und Stimmen der sich äußernden Bewohner in deutlichen Worten, die von den Schülern als Hinweise für die schauspielerische Umsetzung genutzt werden sollen. Dazu müssen mindestens acht (wenn man die Frau des Athleten nicht rechnet) Rollen besetzt werden. Außerdem wird ein Regisseur benötigt, der die Gruppe leitet und berät. Die übrigen Schüler bilden das Publikum der Versammlung in *Arroyo Blanco*. Die Schüler verteilen die Rollen, diskutieren die Darstellung und proben die Szene ein, die anschließend dem Kurs präsentiert und auch evaluiert wird. Je nach Kursgröße kann die Szene von zwei oder drei Gruppen erarbeitet werden.

Acting out the scene of the community meeting about the building of a fence

- Choose one of the following roles:
  Doris Obst
  Jack Jardine
  Jim Shirley
  the athlete
  (his wife)
  Delaney
  Jack Cherrystone
  "a voice"
  person in the crowd
  the director
- Discuss how to present the scene. Read the text carefully and think of gestures, facial expression, intonation.
- Rehearse your interpretation.
- Perform it for your classmates.

104 - 126

Als Hausaufgabe ist zu Kapitel 7 (Teil I) eine *summary* zu erstellen.
Nach dem Vorlesen der Hausaufgabe (*summary* zu *chapter* I.7) werden die Schüler aufgefordert, in arbeitsteiliger Gruppenarbeit auf der Grundlage der Begegnung von Delaney und Jack Jardine im Supermarkt in Kapitel I.7 deren unterschiedliche Positionen zur Einwanderungsproblematik herauszuarbeiten. Je eine Gruppe legt das Augenmerk auf Delaney bzw. Jack Jardine. Anschließend finden sich die Schüler in Paaren aus den unterschiedlichen Gruppen zusammen und tragen sich ihre Ergebnisse gegenseitig vor.

Point out Delaney's and Jack's positions on immigration as voiced in their discussion in the supermarket. (Chapter I.7)

Es kann sich folgendes Tafelbild als Ergebnissicherung des sich anschließenden Plenumsgesprächs ergeben:

Delaney's versus Jack's position on immigration

Delaney

- gate irreconcilable with the foundations of democracy (p. 92, ll. 11 – 15)
- US has always been a nation of grants (p. 93, ll. 1 – 9)
- everyone deserves the chance to assimilate (p. 93, ll. 34 – 36)

Jack Jardine

- there must be a limit to the numbers of immigrants:
  a) immigration a question of national sovereignty (p. 92, l. 28)
  b) US accepted more migrants in one year than all the other countries of the world combined (p. 92, ll. 28 – 30)
  c) illegal migrants are unskilled workers for whom demand is declining (p. 92, ll. 32 – 39)
  d) there are several categories of immigrants (p. 93, ll. 3 – 6)
  e) immigrants cost the taxpayer a lot for social services and they increase the crime rate (p. 93, ll. 13 – 15; ll. 26 – 32)

➡ determination of violently defending his rights

Nachdem Delaneys liberale Einstellung zur Einwanderungsthematik im Gespräch mit Jack Jardine herauskristallisiert wurde, werden die Schüler mit der Frage konfrontiert, ob Delaney sich bei der tatsächlichen Begegnung mit Mexikanern so verhält, wie es seiner Haltung während der Diskussion entspricht. Auf der Grundlage von Kapitel 7 wird die folgende Fragestellung in Form eines *double circle* (Kugellager) bearbeitet. Dabei bilden die Schüler einen Innen- und einen Außenkreis mit gleicher Personenzahl, sodass sich immer zwei Schüler gegenüberstehen. In einem Gespräch mit ihrem Gegenüber kommentieren sie Delaneys Konflikt. Dann rückt der Außenkreis im Uhrzeigersinn weiter, sodass sich neue Dialogpaare für einen erneuten Austausch ergeben.

Comment on the conflict between Delaney's ideal of liberal humanism and his feelings and thoughts when confronted with Mexicans. (Chapter I. 7)

Abschließend können die Ergebnisse stichwortartig an der Tafel/auf Folie festgehalten werden.

Delaney' conflict

Delaney

- maintains a tolerant, democratic position on immigrants during the discussion with Jack Jardine (pp. 92 f.)

versus

- when meeting the Mexican again Delaney feels anger and shame, but does not offer to help him in any way (p. 95)
- in front of his computer Delaney is led into thinking that Cándido threw himself deliberately in front of his car in order to receive money (p. 99)
- seeing the Mexicans' camp he is filled with anger at people littering and intruding on the environment (p. 102) → desire to destroy the camp
- encountering the two Mexicans he wants to escape and have them taken back to their native country to stop them from producing more garbage (p. 105)
- after the car was stolen Delaney imagines Cándido behind the steering wheel of his car (p. 108) → hypocrite

In der Hausaufgabe werden die Schülerinnen und Schüler aufgefordert, die während der Stunde gesammelten Aspekte bezüglich der Einstellungen von Delaney und Jack Jadine zur Einwanderungsthematik aufzuarbeiten:

Write a comment on the conflicting views of Delany and Jack Jardine on Hispanic immigration.

Folgende Ausarbeitung könnte sich z. B. ergeben:

Delaney maintains the ideals of liberal humanism and is a passionate nature-lover. But when he hits the Mexican with his car, he is torn between conflicting feelings toward the man for the first time. On the one hand, he is full of pity and sadness about the man's fate, on the other hand, he loathes the pollution of the environment brought about by the illegal immigrants' camping and living out in the open. He still clings to the idealistic concept of America as a nation of immigrants and therefore vehemently objects to the construction of a gate in front of the property. In his eyes, the gate would exclude many people from the property which would put the residents in an elite-like position. Moreover, in the conversation with Jack Jardine in the supermarket he points out that every immigrant should have a chance to assimilate. When confronted with the Mexican for the second time, however, his former conflict of feelings arises again.
Delaney represents the conflict between his beliefs in an ideal country of immigration and his emotional rejection of the people and circumstances related to the accident.
Jack Jardine takes an unwavering position on the issue of immigration. Although a descendant of immigrants himself, he does not feel like an immigrant any more. Apparently, for him there are several categories of immigrants. He feels justified in

not wanting any more coming into the country and adds a number of reasons for his attitude. Among these is the fact that California is saturated with the huge numbers that have come in the past few years. Another reason is that the illegal immigrants constitute a large group of unskilled workers that are not needed so much any more. Additionally, the costs for the taxpayers in terms of social services and crime related expenses have soared.
Jack stands for the well-off upper-middle-class citizen who feels quite justified in his views and is afraid of being restricted in any way by growing numbers of immigrants. He is determined to use violence to defend his rights.

Develop a word field: "Migration"

migration	language
minority	ethnic group
race	discrimination
education	society

religion	

Word field "Migration" (possible solutions)

migration immigrant/immigration to immigrate into emigrant/emigration to emigrate from/to push-and-pull factors immigration policies a backlash against immigrants person seeking asylum/applicant for asylum/to grant asylum political/racial/religious persecution economic/political refugee influx of illegal immigrants to absorb a new surge of immigrants Green Card naturalization/to naturalize to be granted a work permit	**language** official language language policies institutionalized language English-Only primacy of English resentment toward non-English speakers to eliminate non-English voting ballots to tighten language-proficiency standards language assistance bilingualism/bilingual Spanglish identity/to identify with loss of national unity
minority to be in the minority/majority to outnumber sb integration/segregation to integrate sb into society to encourage/to discourage to adapt to new surroundings to adopt different customs protection of minority rights	**ethnic group** melting pot/salad bowl multiculturalism/multicultural mixed marriages bicultural child ethnic/cultural diversity acculturation Americanization assimilation/to assimilate to cling to one's ethnicity
race Asian, white, black, Native American coloured people multiracial society racial issue/racial tension to carry out a racial policy race relations improve/deteriorate racism/racist/racial hatred/racial bias to hold racist views hate crime racial problems arise race riots break out interracial conflict to persecute/persecution WASP (White Anglo-Saxon Protestant)	**discrimination** to discriminate/to be discriminated against to be/feel superior/inferior to (white) supremacist to have a supremacist attitude toward sb to regard as second-class citizens to live in ghettos (dis)respect/to (dis)respect/(dis)respectful bigotry/bigot privileged/underprivileged disadvantaged (in)tolerance/(in)tolerant to be prejudiced against racial prejudice/bias to discourage prejudice racist/racism xenophobic/xenophobe/xenophobia

education to promote/restrict bilingual programs to raise/to lower the educational level value system cultural heritage	**society** exclusion/to exclude/exclusive education inclusion/to include/inclusive equality/equal (in)justice/(in)just xenophobia/xenophobic
religion Protestant, Catholic, Muslim, Jew Mormon, Baptist denomination to practice a distinctive religion	

How to write an interior monologue

An interior monologue is a narrative technique in fiction that reveals the thoughts passing through the mind of a protagonist.

textual aspects	language support
contents	
feelings thoughts memories associations intuitions worries …	I'm feeling so … I think …/I mean … I can't believe (that) … I'll always remember … That reminds me of … That makes me think (of) … Isn't that …? I sure hope (that) …
structure	
often no chronological, logical order	
style/register	
according to the character's way of speaking (usually) informal: • colloquial, slang words • short forms • filler words	I reckon …/I guess … Wow!/Awesome! God, I hope this damn … I'm so proud of … Well/alright/okay
syntax	
questions exclamations elliptical (incomplete) sentences	Why …?/What will happen? What a …! I No way!/Holy shit!/Yippee! No need to …

Point of View

Whenever an author tells a story there must be a story teller. The story teller is not identical with the author; rather the author chooses a narrator who can tell the story from different angles, i.e. points of view. In the following the three most essential points of view are explained:

I. First-person narrator (limited)
The first-person narrator is a character inside the story He/she can only inform about what he/she knows, feels, thinks and experiences. The narrator can be either a main character or a minor character. Because of the narrator's direct reporting of anything that happens the reader feels as close to the protagonist as the narrator does. It is easy for the reader to identify with the narrator.

II. Third-person narrator (selective-omniscient author)
The third-person author presents things as they are seen through the eyes of one or several characters in the story. He chooses to describe the thoughts and emotions of only one or several characters. The reader does not feel as close to the protagonists because the narrator tells the story in the third-person. He can only identify with those acting persons to whose consciousness the perspective is limited.

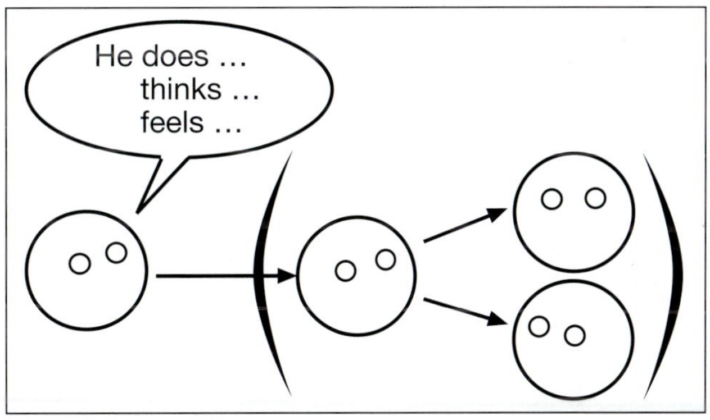

III. Third-person narrator (omniscient author)
An omniscient narrator can move freely in time and space. He can shift from character to character, reporting what he chooses of their speech, actions, thoughts, feelings and emotions. He may give comments or decide to show the action without judgement. This perspective enables the narrator to know everything and to enter the minds of all the characters. The reader can easily identify with the acting persons. But he does not feel spoken to as for instance when a first-person narrator tells a story.

Grafik: Victor Prischtt

Immigration and economic development

Chart 1

Hispanic or Latino Origin Population by Type: 2000 and 2010

(For information on confidentiality protection, nonsampling error, and definitions, see *www.census.gov/prod/en2010/doc/sf1.pdf*)

Origin and type	2000 Number	2000 Percent of total	2010 Number	2010 Percent of total	Change, 2000 to 2010[1] Number	Change, 2000 to 2010[1] Percent
HISPANIC OR LATINO ORIGIN						
Total	281,421,906	100.0	308,745,536	100.0	27,323,632	9.7
Hispanic or Latino	35,305,818	12.5	50,477,594	16.3	15,171,776	43.0
Not Hispanic or Latino	246,116,088	87.5	258,267,944	83.7	12,151,856	4.9
HISPANIC OR LATINO BY TYPE						
Total	35,305,818	100.0	50,477,594	100.0	15,171,776	43.0
Mexican	20,640,711	58.5	31,798,258	63.0	11,157,547	54.1
Puerto Rican	3,406,178	9.6	4,623,716	9.2	1,217,538	35.7
Cuban	1,241,685	3.5	1,785,547	3.5	543,862	43.8
Other Hispanic or Latino	10,017,244	28.4	12,270,073	24.3	2,252,829	22.5
Dominican (Dominican Republic)	764,945	2.2	1,414,703	2.8	649,758	84.9
Central American (excludes Mexican)	1,686,937	4.8	3,998,280	7.9	2,311,343	137.0
Costa Rican	66,588	0.2	126,418	0.3	57,830	84.3
Guatemalan	372,487	1.1	1,044,209	2.1	671,722	180.3
Honduran	217,569	0.6	633,401	1.3	415,832	191.1
Nicaraguan	177,684	0.5	348,202	0.7	170,518	96.0
Panamanian	91,723	0.3	165,456	0.3	73,733	80.4
Salvadoran	655,165	1.9	1,648,968	3.3	993,803	151.7
Other Central American[2]	103,721	0.3	31,626	0.1	−72,095	−69.5
South American	1,353,562	3.8	2,769,434	5.5	1,415,872	104.6
Argentinean	100,864	0.3	224,952	0.4	124,088	123.0
Bolivian	42,068	0.1	99,210	0.2	57,142	135.8
Chilean	68,849	0.2	126,810	0.3	57,961	84.2
Colombian	470,684	1.3	908,734	1.8	438,050	93.1
Ecuadorian	260,559	0.7	564,631	1.1	304,072	116.7
Paraguayan	8,769	—	20,023	—	11,254	128.3
Peruvian	233,926	0.7	531,358	1.1	297,432	127.1
Uruguayan	18,804	0.1	56,884	0.1	38,080	202.5
Venezuelan	91,507	0.3	215,023	0.4	123,516	135.0
Other South American[3]	57,532	0.2	21,809	—	−35,723	−62.1
Spaniard	100,135	0.3	635,253	1.3	535,110	534.4
All other Hispanics or Latino[4]	6,111,665	17.3	3,452,403	6.8	−2,659,262	−43.5

– Percentage rounds to 0.0.

[1] The observed changes in Hispanic origin counts between Census 2000 and the 2010 Census could be attributed to a number or factors. Demographic change since 2000, which includes births and deaths in a geographic area and migration in and out of a geographic area, will have an impact on the resulting 2010 Census counts. Some changes in the Hispanic origin question's wording and format since Census 2000 could have influenced reporting patterns. In the 2010 Census. Additionally, changes to the Hispanic origin edit and coding procedures could have impacted the 2010 counts. These factors should especially be considered when observing changes for detailed Hispanic groups.

[2] This category includes people who reported Central Américan Indian groups, "Canal Zone," and "Central Américan."

[3] This category includes people who reported South Américan Indian groups and "South Américan."

[4] This category includes people who reported "Hispanic" or "Latino" and other general terms.

Datenerhebung: U.S. Census Bureau. *Census 2000 Summary File 1* and *2010 Census Summary File 1.*

Chart 2

Emigration and Return Migration Rate of Mexican Residents, 2006 to 2011

Datenerhebung: INEGI, Estimates based on Mexico's National Occupation and Employment Survey (Encuesta Nacional de Ocupación y Emploe, ENOE), 2012

Chart 3

Average Annual Real GDP Growth in Mexico and the United States 1985 – 2009

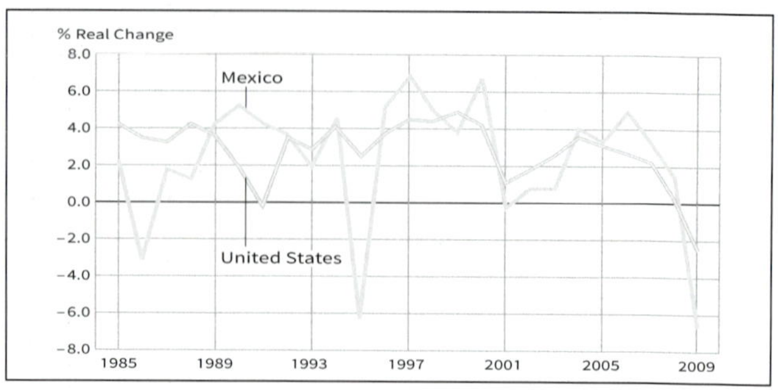

Datenerhebung: Congressional Research Service

Proportion of Hispanics

Chart 4

Percent Distribution of the Hispanic Population by State: 2010
(For more information on confidentiality protection, nonsampling error, and definitions, see *www.census.gov/prod/cen2010/doc/sf1.pdf)*

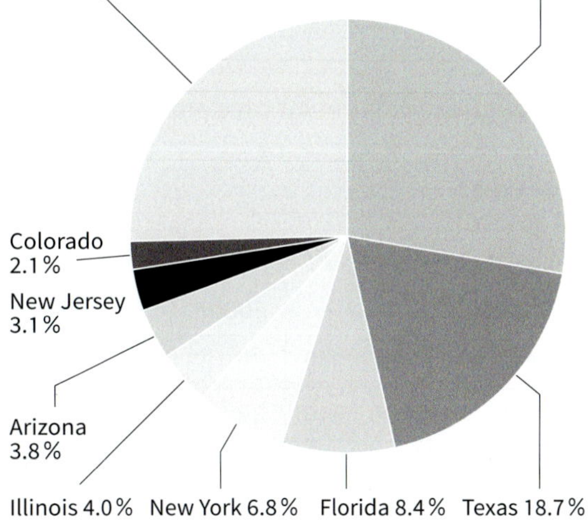

Datenerhebung: U. S. Census Bureau, *2010 Census Summary File 1.*

Chart 5

Hispanic or Latino Population as a Percent of Total Population by County: 2010
(For more information on confidentiality protection, nonsampling error, and definitions, see *www.census.gov/prod/en2010/doc/sf1.pdf)*

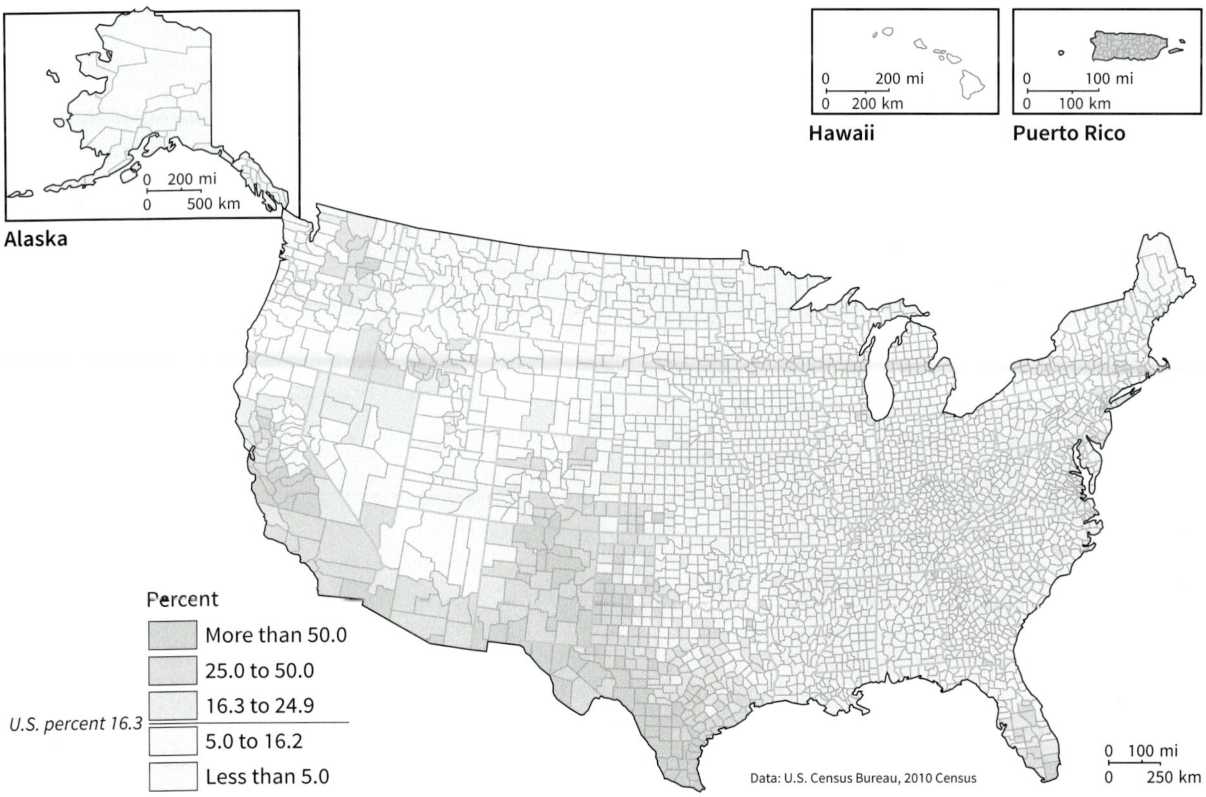

Datenerhebung: U.S. Census Bureau, Census 2000 Summary File 1 and 2010 Summary File

1. Describe the development of Hispanic immigration into the USA (chart 1).
2. Explain the development of the number of people departing from Mexico and returning to Mexico in relation with the development of the gross domestic product (GDP) in Mexico between 2006 and 2007 (charts 2 and 3).
3. Comment on the proportion of Mexican immigrants in the states (charts 4 and 5).

Analysis of tables/graphs/charts

There are different types of presentation of statistical data:

Various types	General aspects

Census Population by Age

Age	2010	2000	1990
15–24	43,626,342	39,183,891	36,774,327
25–34	41,063,948	39,891,724	43,175,932
35–44	41,070,606	45,148,527	37,578,903
45–54	45,006,716	37,677,952	25,223,086

A table provides data as the basis for analysis and is presented in the form of a grid with numbers arranged in lines and columns. It aims to present data in a structured way, thereby making it easy to understand the information.

- How trustworthy is the source?
- Are the numbers that are given topical?
- Are the figures absolute numbers or percentage figures – and what is the function of this kind of presentation?
- What do the given data suggest?
- Take into consideration why a chart/graph/table has been chosen as the means of visual representation.
- Turn the percentage figures/data into words and compare them.
- Relate the given data to the context in question.

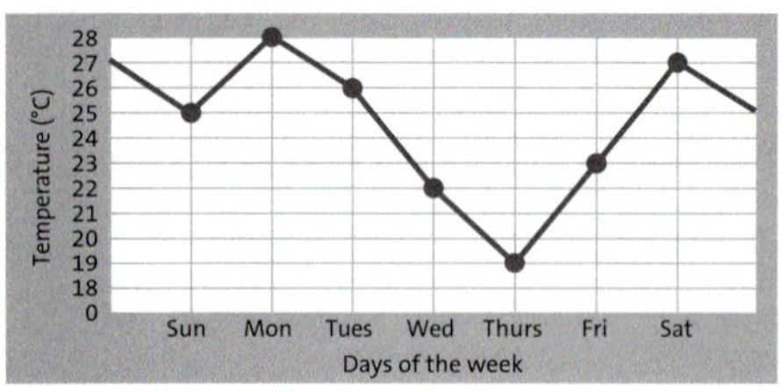

A (line) graph presents one or more lines in a system of coordinates/axes – a horizontal and a vertical axis. It presents the development of figures/variables over a period of time.

Useful terms and phrases

• to reach a peak/a low point/an all-time high/low of ... • to remain constant • to go through a period of growth • to increase/rise/go up/grow • to decrease/fall/drop/go downs fall/decline/drop/decrease • an increase/a rise/growth • to grow ... by 30 %/at a certain rate a rise of 3 %/in expenses/to $ 66 • steep/strong/rapid ... growth • a gradual/steady/permanent ... fall • a slight/hardly noticeable ... rise/fall

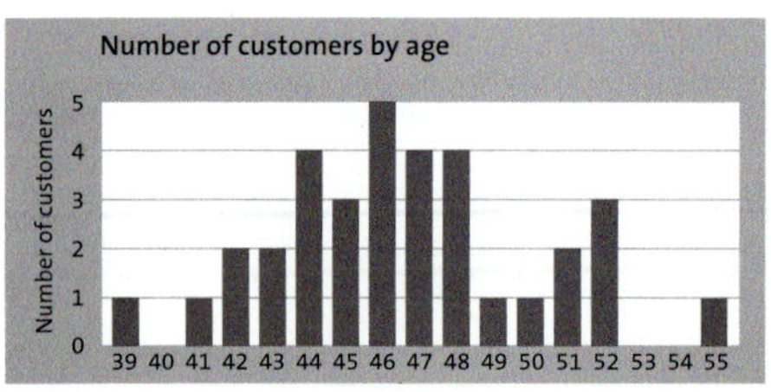

A bar chart provides differences between various things. It presents bars of different heights in a system of coordinates. The bars can be arranged horizontally or vertically.

Useful terms and phrases

• in comparison with • in contrast to • to achieve an average/below-average/above-average figure • to be at the top/bottom of the ranking • to rank first/second/third ... last
• the highest/lowest figure/scores • no/little/a big difference between A and B (... regarding ... last year ...)
• the figures are identical/similar to ... • the vast majority of only a minority ... • to experience a sudden rise/drop after a brief interval of recovery

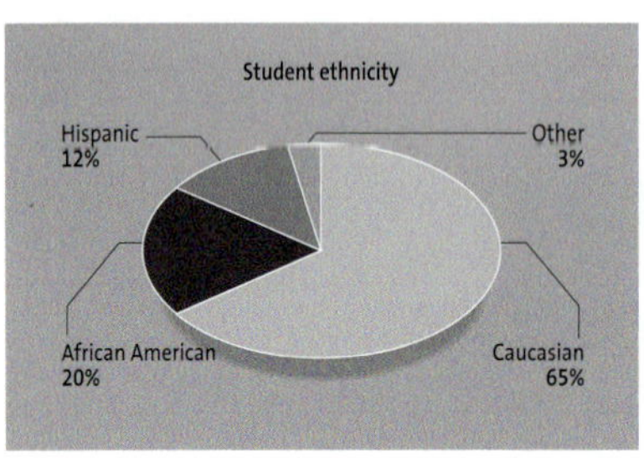

A pie chart presents percentages of a whole. It consists of a circle/pie separated into different segments.

Useful terms and phrases

• the pie chart is divided into ... • segments/sections ...
• each section represents ... • the share of 16 % of the total amount is about 20 million people • the biggest/the smallest section ... • the whole circle stands for ...
• the chart shows the share of ... • percentage-wise • a marginal percentage of ... • an incredibly big amount of ...

While-reading task part 1, chapter 1

Answer the following questions in complete sentences. Indicate the page(s) and line(s) where you found the answer.

1. Where does Delaney Mossbacher live?

____

2. Delaney has the backseat of his car full of newspapers, mayonnaise jars and cans. Why?

____

3. What are the first two things Delaney thinks of after the accident?

____

4. How do the other drivers react to the accident?

____

5. Is the victim of the accident hurt?

____

6. Why is Delaney not able to really speak with the victim?

____

7. What kind of help does the victim ask for?

____

8. Why does the Mexican refuse to see a doctor?

____

9. Delaney thinks the Mexican lives in Topanga State Park, a state property. What does this idea make him feel?

____

10. For how long has Delaney been living in Los Angeles?

____

11. In what way does Delaney lie to his car dealer?

____

12. What part of Delaney's car is being fixed at the Acura dealer?

____

While-reading task part 1, chapter 2

Right or wrong? Correct the wrong statements and indicate the page(s) and lines(s) where you found the answers.

	right	wrong	p., l.
1. In the morning before the accident Cándido does not have breakfast.			
2. Cándido is hurt so badly by Delaney's car that he can hardly move.			
3. América takes the bus to Venice to go shopping.			
4. América makes sure nobody follows her.			
5. When he was a little boy, Cándido lived in Guatemala.			
6. Cándido refuses to see a doctor because he fears legal problems.			
7. Cándido was eight years old when his mother died.			
8. América cries because Cándido is so drunk that he cannot remember her name.			
9. América is 17 years old and pregnant.			
10. Since Cándido is too sick to work, he is happy that América wants to look for a job.			
11. Cándido and América have been living in the canyon for three weeks.			

I While-reading tasks part 1, chapter 3

Fill in the missing words in this summary. Indicate the page(s) and line(s) where you found the answer.

Delaney goes through his morning ritual of preparing (1) ____________________ (__________) for his family. After Kyra has joined her husband and son in the kitchen, they hear a scream from the backyard – a (2) ____________________ (__________) has managed to seize one of their (3) ____________________ (__________). They try to pursue the fleeing animal up the (4) ____________________ (__________) but they do not succeed in getting hold of it. In the evening there is a (5) ____________________ (__________) of the residents of Arroyo Blanco Estates because some of them want to erect a (6) ____________________ (__________) in front of the estate. There is a heated debate about this issue. Delaney wants to express his (7) ____________________ (__________) of people feeding coyotes but only makes a pathetic impression. After Delaney has left the meeting he meets the (8) ____________________ (__________) of one of the strong supporters of the gate who asks him about the (9) ____________________ (__________).

II While reading assignments Part 1, chapter 4

Complete the following sentences and indicate the page(s) and line(s) where you found the answer.

1. América climbs up out of the canyon in order ____________________
2. Cándido's reaction to América's leaving is not happy, but ____________________
3. While América is not with him in the canyon, Cándido thinks about ____________________
4. When América asks "Did children bear children?" she means that ____________________
5. The people at the labour exchange are mostly ____________________
6. The men that approach Cándido do not have friendly intentions because ____________________

   ____
7. For Cándido and América, the message ("Beaners die") of the gringos who destroyed their camp represents a menace because ____________________

   ____

   ____

While-reading task part 1, chapter 5

Indicate the page(s) and line(s) where the text says that ...

1. ... living in a remote location like Arroyo Blanco makes Delaney feel happy.

   ____

2. ... Delaney reconsiders the possible advantages of the gate. ____________________________
3. ... Kyra regrets having insisted on her husband telling her the truth about Sacheverell.

   ____

4. ... Kyra thinks the bathroom in the Matzoob's house is not modem enough to sell it.

   ____

5. ... experience in her business has taught Kyra not to judge potential house buyers by their looks.

   ____

6. ... Jordan is not too upset about the dog's deaths. ____________________________
7. ... Kyra's aspiration for the future is to be her own boss. ____________________________
8. ... Delaney wants to forget Sacheverell's death and move on with his life.

   ____

While-reading task part 1, chapter 6

Tick off the correct ending of the sentences and indicate the page(s) and line(s) where the text says so.

1. América accuses Cándido of not being able to take control of their situation because
   a) he behaves like a lazy Mexican "macho".
   b) she is frustrated and afraid of their future.
   c) she is tired of eating beans and tortilla every day.
2. América thinks having accepted the coffee from the Mexican was a mistake because
   a) she senses he is a dangerous person.
   b) it tastes awfully sweet.
   c) coffee will harm her baby.
3. At the labor exchange, América feels entitled to getting the job instead of Mary because
   a) she had been waiting longer than Mary.
   b) Mary looks too elegant for the job.
   c) she does not speak English.
4. Since the teenagers have destroyed their camp, Cándido has to find a new, safe place for them. When he sees a perfect place to camp in the canyon, he does not feel his pain and
   a) falls deeply asleep.
   b) dreams of his home in Mexico.
   c) builds a rock fireplace.
5. Cándido lies to the man with the strange eyes about the water in the canyon because
   a) he does not want any more illegal immigrants to camp there.
   b) he is worried about the man's safety.
   c) he fears the stranger will pollute the water.
6. At the parking lot of the Chinese store, the Americans' reaction to the sight of Cándido is
   a) cheerful friendliness.
   b) fearful disgust.
   c) thoughtless indifference.
7. América has been working hard and for two hours longer, but she is happy because
   a) her boss is not there.
   b) she will get more money.
   c) Candelario Pérez will give her another job.
8. Mary lives
   a) in a rather poor, but welcoming neighborhood.
   b) on the canyon road.
   c) in a small bungalow in Arroyo Blanco.
9. Her boss takes América back to the labor exchange, but
   a) does not pay her.
   b) does not hire her for the next day.
   c) does not pay her for the extra hours she worked.

While-reading task part 1, chapter 7

Answer the following questions in complete sentences. Indicate the page(s) and line(s) where you found the answer.

1. Why is Delaney in such a hurry when he wants to buy pasta at the supermarket?

2. How does Jack Jardine justify his approval of the gate?

3. What is Delaney' attitude towards the United States controlling its borders?

4. Which costs does Jack Jardine mention that the immigrants are costing the American tax payer?

5. Does Kyra sell the Da Ros house to Louisa and Bill Greutert?

6. What is the reason for Delaney not being able to concentrate on writing his column about the species of the canyon?

7. On his hike in the canyon Delaney discovers two dirty sleeping bags and a lot of trash. What is his reaction?

8. Why does Delaney feel scared when he hears the two voices on his hike in the canyon?

9. After his encounter with José Navidad and his friend in the canyon, Delaney notices that his car is not at the spot where he had parked it. What is his first explanation?

10. Who does Delaney blame when he realizes that his car is stolen?

While-reading task part 1, chapter 8

This is a summary of Chapter 8. Find the correct order of the sentences.

1	Scraping the statues is very painful for América because the corrosive cleaning materials hurt her hands and the fumes give her a headache.
2	Since América is very hungry after a day of hard work, she buys some food at the supermarket and eats it right there.
3	When Cándido is not where they had agreed to meet (at the supermarket), América hopes that he has found a job.
4	Cándido leads América to their new camp, where they happily feast on the food they bought with the money she has earned scrubbing buddhas.
5	Finally, América decides to go back to their camp by herself.
6	At the end of the day, her boss takes América back to the labor exchange in his car (without putting his hand in her lap), pays her 25$ and leaves.
7	Cándido is waiting for América at the supermarket's parking lot, careful not to be noticed by the American customers.
8	Even though Cándido feels stronger, he is not accepted for a job, but América is hired for another day of scrubbing buddhas.
9	On her way back to their camp, América is raped by José Navidad.
10	The next morning Cándido and América are the first ones at the labor exchange, hoping for a job.

Correct order: __7__ ______ ______ ______ ______ ______ ______ ______ ______ ______

Component 2

Cándido's and América's best of all worlds

Zu Beginn der Arbeit mit ***Component 2*** sollten die Schülerinnen und Schüler aufgefordert werden, Part 2 parallel zu der Arbeit an Part 1 zu lesen und dabei die am Ende dieses *Components* zur Verfügung gestellten *Copies* mit den unterschiedlichen *while-reading*-Aufgaben zu bearbeiten (***Copies 14–20***).

2.1 Symbolism

Boyle benutzt in *The Tortilla Curtain* auf verschiedenen Ebenen Symbole, um der Geschichte von Delaney und Cándido Nachdruck zu verleihen. Am auffälligsten dürften dabei die *telling names* sein, die sich in seinem Roman finden. Es ist daher nötig, die Schülerinnen und Schüler darauf aufmerksam zu machen, dass die Namen der Protagonisten nicht zufällig gewählt wurden.

Der Name der weißen Hauptpersonen, Delaney und Kyra Mossbacher, muss sicherlich erläutert werden. Boyle selbst definierte in einem Interview „Mossbacher" folgendermaßen: *„A mossback in the Américan language is someone who is a sort of stick-in-the-mud conservative who doesn't think for himself much ..."* (pointed out by Prof. Freese; can be found in: Erica Jong and T. Coraghessan Boyle, *Zwei Interviews*. Paderborn: Paderborner Universitätsreden 64, 1998, p. 24). Die Schülerinnen und Schüler sollten ausgehend von dieser Definition zu erklären versuchen, inwiefern dieser Name auf Delaney passt.

In view of Boyle's definition of a mossbach, why do you think he has chosen this name for Delaney?

Although Delaney calls himself a liberal humanist, it becomes clear that his liberalism is more of an attitude than a belief. He finds himself worrying about his car first and not the human victim of the accident, and it turns out that he can be influenced easily by his wife and friends.

Je nachdem wie weit die Schülerinnen und Schüler den Roman gelesen haben, kann sich eine Diskussion darüber entwickeln, ob Delaney wirklich liberal ist oder nicht. Im Verlauf der Besprechung des Romans wird dieser Aspekt immer wieder auftauchen.

Während Mossbach erläutert werden muss, können die Schülerinnen und Schüler sicherlich zu einigen anderen Namen im Roman spontan in einem *think-pair-share*-Verfahren Stellung nehmen. Dabei sollten Vermutungen über die Bedeutung von Cándidos Namen zurückgestellt werden.

What can you say about some of the other names in *The Tortilla Curtain*?

América stands for both Americas, the southern part where a lot of poor people live and the northern part where these people desperately try to find a better life. **José Navidad**, the rapist, stands for the Spanish conquerors who came to the

America of the Indians and deprived them of everything they had, ironically his name means Christmas.
Jack **Cherrystone**, Doris **Obst** and Jack **Jardine** (jardin = garden in French) have names that refer to nature and gardens.
Also the fact that Jack Jardine's son has got the same name as his father suggests that there is not only a likeness in names, but that they have the same opinions and share the same political ideas.
Resurrección, Cándido's first wife, remains childless although her name suggests a renewing of life.

Beim weiteren Lesen sollten diese symbolischen Namen im Auge behalten werden. Wir lesen in Zeile 5 auf S. 178, dass América indianischer Abstammung ist, d. h. sie gehört zu den Ureinwohnern Amerikas (*„Indita. She hated it when he called her that: his little Indian“*). Ebenso treffen wir später auf Dominick Flood, der den Namen einer Naturgewalt trägt, was zu ihm passt, da er ein Verbrecher ist. Dies muss hier noch nicht erwähnt werden, da die Schülerinnen und Schüler ein *Worksheet* bekommen, auf dem sie laufend die Erkenntnisse eintragen können.

Im weiteren Verlauf des Unterrichtsgesprächs können die Schülerinnen und Schüler dazu aufgefordert werden, Assoziationen zu „Cándido“ zu äußern. Dabei könnten Latein-/Spanischschülerinnen und -schüler auf die Bedeutung *white* kommen, vom Autor wurde jedoch „Candide“, der Held des gleichnamigen Romans von Voltaire, als Vorbild und Namensgeber seines Cándido genannt (pointed out by Prof. Freese, in *Zwei Interviews*, p. 30). Vermutlich sind die Schülerinnen und Schüler diesem Roman noch nicht begegnet, daher bietet sich als Hausaufgabe an, sich über dieses Werk zu informieren.

Find out what "Candide" by Voltaire is about and what kind of character Candide is. Explain why Cándido was named after him.

Candide is about a young man who sets out to find the best of all possible worlds. Voltaire wanted to refute Leibnitz' idea of a "best of all possible worlds" by writing this rather ridiculous account of his hero's pursuit of happiness. Candide meets all kinds of evil people and has to deal with numerous dangerous situations, he suffers all the bad luck possibly to be had, but still clings to his belief in the best of all worlds. The similarity between this 18th-century character and Boyle's Cándido is obvious. Where Candide is looking for the best of all worlds introduced to him by his philosophy teacher, Cándido is searching for happiness in the USA. Both encounter terrible situations and keep failing in the pursuit of success. However, Boyle's Cándido does not desire the best of all worlds, just a better life than the one he has in Mexico.

Bei der Namensgebung der Haustiere im Haushalt der Mossbachers erlaubt sich Boyle einen Scherz mit Kyra, die er hier als Intellektuelle darstellt, die ihren Hunden und ihrer Katze bedeutsame Namen gibt. Man kann die Enträtselung dieser Namen ebenfalls als Hausaufgabe geben, dann sollte man jedoch den Nachnamen von Dame Edith, Osbert and Sacheverell dazu nennen, nämlich Sitwell. Falls mit der Schöningh-Ausgabe des Romans gearbeitet wird, kann auf die in den *annotations* gegebenen Informationen zurückgegriffen werden.

Find out who Dame Edith, Osbert an Sacheverell were.

Dame Edith Sitwell (1887–1964) was a well-known poet, her younger brothers Osbert and Sacheverell were also known for their writings, Osbert as a poet, essayist and novelist and Sacheverell as an art historian. They constituted one of the most extraordinary literary families in the England of their time.

Als Hilfestellung für die Schülerinnen und Schüler kann man ihnen ***Copy 13*** austeilen, auf der sie die Ergebnisse der Namensuntersuchungen eintragen können. Außerdem sollen sie aufgefordert werden, im Verlauf der Lektüre neue Erkenntnisse hinzuzufügen, z. B. über Américas Herkunft und über Dominick Flood.
Nach Besprechung der Namen der Charaktere des Romans sollte man ebenso die Bezeichnung des Wohnkomplexes, in dem die Mossbachers leben, kurz untersuchen. Die Schülerinnen und Schüler sollten Seite 33 nochmals lesen.

Comment on the name and appearance of the Mossbacher's community, namely Arroyo Blanco, which is also the title of Part One.

Arroyo Blanco means white brook in Spanish. It is quite ironic that the expensive, exclusively white neighbourhood has got a Spanish name. Also the appearance of the homes is uniformly the same, they are all of Spanish Mission style, and even the colours are described with Spanish/Indian expressions ("Rancho White with Navajo trim", p. 33).
The aim of the whites living in this Hispanic-looking area is to keep all minorities, especially the Hispanics, out of their premises.
By calling part one Arroyo Bianco Boyle points out this irony from the start.

Nachdem im ersten *Component* die einzelnen Personen mit ihren unterschiedlichen Wünschen und Meinungen untersucht wurden, soll das Augenmerk der Schülerinnen und Schüler nun auf die Vergangenheit der Charaktere gelenkt werden. Dabei bieten sich América und Cándido an, da über die Vergangenheit der Mossbachers wenig berichtet wird. Vor der Besprechung sollte als Hausaufgabe *Chapter I,4* nochmals gelesen worden sein.
Bei genauer Betrachtung von Cándidos Lebensgeschichte zeigen sich Parallelen zu alttestamentarischen Geschichten, auf die die Schülerinnen und Schüler in einem Unterrichtsgespräch vermutlich gestoßen werden müssen. Daher empfiehlt sich ein Tafelbild zur Zusammenfassung der Ergebnisse.

What do we learn about Cándido's and América's past? (Chapter I,4)

p. 49	Cándido has known América since she was four, he married her older sister Resurrección, he worked in the north for nine months, was home for three, made a lot of money
pp. 51f.	after seven years his wife left him for another man, América brings him the bad news, "Then came his season in hell" (p. 51, l. 3)
p. 51	Cándido started drinking, he met América again and changed, still not as successful as before

Can you think of any stories that Cándido's life reminds you of?

There are two stories from the Bible mingled with this lifestory. On the one hand, there is Joseph's story with seven good and seven bad years, on the other hand, there is the story of his father Jacob who was tricked into first marrying Laban's older daughter Rachel and then her younger sister Leah.

Can you find other instances where Boyle refers to biblical scenes?

Delaney's stepson Jordan plays with his Nintendo and Delaney refers to the game as an "electronic Armageddon" thus foreshadowing the real Armageddon (p. 94, ll. 23 f.).

Cándido compares himself to Job (p. 109), the classic case of someone enduring pain inflicted on him by God in order to test his faith (Book of Job, Old Testament). By saying that even Job would have broken down under these circumstances, Cándido admits that he is losing his faith in God.

Um auf weitere Symbole in diesem Roman hinzuweisen, sollten die Schülerinnen und Schüler nochmals die Szene laut lesen oder von der CD hören, in der Sacheverell von einem Kojoten gerissen wird (p. 38, l. 20). „There was a silence, ...“ – p. 41, l. 7. Danach wird im Unterrichtsgespräch erörtert, ob es hierbei wirklich nur um Kojoten geht.

Explain what Sacheverell's capture stands for.

Sacheverell is called "The poor dog. It couldn't have defended itself from a rabbit." (p. 40, l. 9) This shows that he has been changed by civilisation so much that he can no longer do what dogs are meant to do, e.g. chase rabbits. Wildlife in the form of a coyote, attracted by people in the first place, has taken his life without hesitation, taking what by natural law was its right to take.
Delaney himself has no chance of retrieving the dog because he has not got the ability to race a coyote. So the coyote proves to be the most reckless and fastest, leaving behind a terrified civilisation: "... mother and son, huddled in Jordan's narrow bed with Osbert and Dame Edith, looking like survivors of a shipwreck adrift on a raft." (p. 1, ll. 42 – 44)
So the human beings and their pets have tried to escape crime: "Crime? Up here? Wasn't that what they'd come here to escape?" (p. 44, ll. 1 f.) to find that there are other dangers to be avoided: "... and there it was, wild nature ..." (p. 39, l. 1).
The reader can notice the parallels: Sacheverell stands for the whites and their lifestyle, the coyote stands for the poor Mexicans intruding and trying to participate in some of the whites' wealth.

Diese Parallele zwischen den Kojoten und den Mexikanern wird in dem Roman immer wieder aufgegriffen und sollte von den Schülerinnen und Schülern daher im Blick behalten werden. So wird der zweite Hund, Osbert, ebenfalls von einem Kojoten geholt, obwohl der Zaun inzwischen höher gemacht wurde, und Dame Edith wird von Cándido und América im dritten Teil verspeist.

Dazu teilen sich je vier Schüler ein Blatt (*placemat*), auf dem sie ihre Ideen in dem ihnen zugeteilten Schreibbereich notieren, das Blatt drehen, die Einträge der Mitschüler lesen, ergänzen, kommentieren und sich schließlich auf die wichtigsten Aspekte einigen, die in der Mitte des Blattes festgehalten werden. Im anschließenden Plenum wird in etwa folgendes Folienbild entwickelt, das die Schüler übernehmen und im Laufe der Lektüre ergänzen.

Mexicans	**Coyotes**
• live in canyon	• live in canyon eat heartily among the rocks and the waste places (p. 74)
• are believed to steal cars	• hunting, gamboling, stealing (p. 74)
• eat Dame Edith in Part Three (p. 275)	• eat dogs (p. 38, p. 169)

2.2 América – everybody's victim

Nach der Lektüre des ersten Teils ist den Schülerinnen und Schülern klar, dass die Mexikaner ihre Heimat verlassen und all die Strapazen auf sich nehmen, um ihren Traum vom besseren Leben in den USA zu verwirklichen. Um den Kontrast zwischen Traum und Wirklichkeit herauszustellen, sollten die Schülerinnen und Schüler nach erneuter häuslicher Lektüre des zweiten Kapitels von Teil I die Lebensbedingungen von América und Cándido und ihren Traum beschreiben können. Die Ergebnisse dieser Hausaufgabe könnten in einem Tafelbild festgehalten werden.

Read chapter two (part one) again and describe in a few sentences the contrast between América's and Cándido's dreams and their living conditions.

Living conditions:

- they have a camp in a canyon by a streambed (p. 22)
- it is eight miles from this canyon to the labour exchange → work (p. 22)
- canyon is full of shrubs with thorns, snakes and spiders along the path to the highway (p. 23)
- they sleep on blankets in the sand (p. 27)
- they drink water from stream and have to make a fire every time they want to cook (p. 24)
- they move about in eternal fear of being stopped by the police (p. 23)
- after the accident Cándido cannot see a doctor despite his severe injuries; the only remedies they can afford are some food including meat, aspirin, alcohol and some Band-Aids (p. 25)

➡ they live like fugitives under dreadful circumstances without any prospect of improvement

Dreams:

- América describes her dream herself: "A house, a yard, maybe a TV and a car, too – nothing fancy, no palaces like the ***gringos*** built – just four walls and a roof." (p. 31, ll. 29 – 31)

Die Realität für die Mexikaner wird jedoch immer bedrohlicher; am Ende von *part one* wird América von einem Landsmann vergewaltigt. Diese Vergewaltigung kommt nicht als Überraschung für den Leser, da Boyle sie bereits vorbereitet hat. Die Schülerinnen und Schüler sollten in einer Gruppenarbeit herausfinden, inwiefern eine Atmosphäre der Bedrohung für América aufgebaut wurde. Die Ergebnisse können von den Schülerinnen und Schülern auf Folie festgehalten und anschließend bei ihrer Präsentation diskutiert werden.

América's rape has been foreshadowed. Find examples in the previous chapters of part one that hint at this event and make the reader anticipate that something awful will happen.

- ... his wife, a barefoot girl from the country who didn't know a thing about the world, out there among all those men, those lowlifes who'd do anything for a buck – or a woman ... (p. 29)
- ... he'd warn América to douse the fire and keep out of sight (p. 30)
- Cándido remembers a twelve-year-old girl in Tijuana who was raped by a gang of men (p. 30)
- ... outlined the wickedness of the gabacho world and the perfidy of his fellow braceros at the labour exchange (p. 49)
- p. 57.: The men were staring at her openly now, and their stares were harder, hungrier. ...
- They were starving and she was fresh meat. (p. 57)
- ... looming nightmarishly, was the faces of those animals at the border – Mexican animals – the ones who'd come out of the night to attack her and Cándido as they crossed over. (p. 57)
- ... they went for her. A knife was in her face, their hands were all over her, and they jerked the clothes from her as if skinning a rabbit ... (p. 57)
- América meets the future rapist, he offers her coffee and she accepts. (p. 75)
- ... there was something rotten inside of him (p. 77)
- This was bad. This man was bad. ... she knew he was crazy, loco, demented ... (p. 77)
- And when the fat man laid his hand casually across her thigh, ... she wanted to fling it away from her ... She just let it lie there like a dead thing, though it moved and insinuated itself and she wanted to scream for the car to stop. (p. 89)

Nach dieser intensiven Beschäftigung mit América sollten die Schülerinnen und Schüler durch eine *creative writing*-Aufgabe dazu motiviert werden, in Américas Gemütszustand einzutauchen. Dabei eignet sich ein innere Monolog, allerdings ist von einem Bezug zum Tag der Vergewaltigung abzusehen. Es bietet sich an, América den ersten Arbeitstag und das darauf folgende Festmahl und ihre Gefühle während dieses Tages (Angst vor den Männern am *labour exchange* – Mary – die harte Arbeit – Ekel vor der Hand des Patrón – Kaufrausch – romantische Situation mit Cándido) reflektieren zu lassen. Die Schülerinnen und Schüler sollten dafür nochmals Kapitel 6 und 8 bis S. 113, l. 41 lesen.

Unterstützung sowohl zum Zieltextformat des inneren Monologs als auch in sprachlicher Hinsicht finden die Schüler auf ***Copy 2***. Es ist natürlich auch denkbar, diese Aspekte von den Schülern selbst zusammentragen zu lassen.

Put yourself into América's position on the evening of her first workday and write down her feelings and thoughts in an interior monologue.

Telling Names

Make notes to sum up your findings of the telling names in this novel and explain their function. Keep this list and add any new names or explanations.

Mossbacher: ____________________

América: ____________________

Cándido: ____________________

José Navidad: ____________________

Jack Jardine: ____________________

Jack Cherrystone: ____________________

Doris Obst: ____________________

Dame Edith: ____________________

Osbert: ____________________

Sacheverell: ____________________

Telling Names – solutions

Make notes to sum up your findings of the telling names in this novel and explain their function. Keep this list and – add – any new names or explanations.

Mossbacher:	mossback = conservative who does not think for himself Delaney is influenced easily
América:	stands for both Americas is the true America raped by Spanish conquerors
Cándido:	like Voltaire's Candide he is looking for a better life Boyle shows how futile this search is by giving him this name
José Navidad:	his name means Christmas which does not fit his very unattractive character
Jack Jardine:	his last name suggest a garden metaphor the fact that his son has the same name shows that they both share the same opinions
Jack Cherrystone:	his name also hints at gardening
Doris Obst:	her name also suggests gardens and nature all three represent the majority of white people who want to flee from big-city life, but are confronted with wildlife they cannot handle
Dame Edith:	poet (1887 – 1964)
Osbert:	younger brother of Edith, poet, essayist, novelist
Sacheverell:	art historian by naming her pets after the members of this literary family, Kyra is trying to be considered an intellectual

While-reading assignments part 2, chapter 1

Answer the following questions – make sentences.

1. What is a slim Jim?

2. What is the most annoying thing about Kenny Grissom?

3. What is the American Way?

4. What makes Kyra so angry after lunch?

5. Why is Kyra concerned about the group of Mexican men standing on Ventura Boulevard?

6. What other dangerous animals apart from coyotes are there near the Mossbachers' home?

7. Kyra finds a shopping cart near one of the mansions she tries to sell. What explanations for its being there can she think of?

8. Kyra confronts a man the second time that day. Describe the differences between the two encounters.

While-reading assignments part 2, chapter 2

What do they think?

1. p. 147, l. 41: police officers

2. p. 149, l. 15: The man

3. p. 149, l. 42: Graciela

4. p. 150, l. 18: Resurreción

5. p. 150, l. 45: A woman

6. p. 152, l. 44: Al Lopez

7. p. 153, l. 14: she (América)

8. p. 158, l. 22: Al Lopez

While-reading assignments part 2, chapter 3

Right or wrong? Correct the wrong statements.

	right	wrong
1. Delaney's life feels good again as he prepares Sunday dinner.		
2. Kyra has had no success in removing the Mexicans from the 7-Eleven on Shoup.		
3. Kyra has no problem with Mexicans taking advantage of California's welfare system.		
4. Dominick Flood knows Delaney's column in *Wide Open Space*.		
5. Jim Shirley tells the men at the meeting that they should not worry about burglaries.		
6. The purpose of the meeting at Dominick Flood's house is to decide on building a wall around their development.		
7. Flood must wear an electronic device on his ankle so that he cannot leave his house because he has attacked a man.		
8. Dominick Flood has used his contacts to make sure that the labour exchange will be closed for good.		
9. A coyote tries to overcome the new fence but is stopped by it.		

Corrections:

While-reading assignments part 2, chapter 4

Tick off the correct ending of the sentences.

1. Cándido is cheated by
   - □ a) a friend from Mexico.
   - □ b) América.
   - □ c) his new boss.
2. Cándido enjoys a meal of
   - □ a) fish caught in the creek.
   - □ b) birds caught and fried.
   - □ c) fresh vegetables bought at the market.
3. When Cándido reaches the labour exchange the next morning
   - □ a) nobody is there.
   - □ b) his friends greet him.
   - □ c) he finds work right away.
4. Cándido is frustrated because
   - □ a) his new job is awful.
   - □ b) the closing of the labor exchange puts an end to his dreams of legal life in the US.
   - □ c) he has lost his money.
5. Cándido sees a purse in an open car and
   - □ a) steals it.
   - □ b) considers stealing it.
   - □ c) knows that he would never steal it.
6. When Cándido tells América that he wants to go to Canoga Park on his own
   - □ a) she refuses to be left back in the canyon.
   - □ b) she is glad that he does not expect her to come with him.
   - □ c) she suggests that she can go he stays back.
7. After the walk to the top of their canyon
   - □ a) América is excited about the view over San Fernando Valley.
   - □ b) Cándido is totally exhausted.
   - □ c) América is totally exhausted.
8. In Canoga Park
   - □ a) there are many Hispanic people on the street.
   - □ b) nobody speaks Spanish.
   - □ c) the houses are adorable and rich people seem to live there.
9. The job situation at Canoga Park's labor exchange is
   - □ a) much better.
   - □ b) bad because of the recession.
   - □ c) has not changed.

While-reading assignments part 2, chapter 6

This is a summary of chapter 6. Find the correct order of the sentences.

	Kyra and Delaney end up quarreling after dinner and do not make up in the following days.
	It turns out that the Mexican delivers fliers inviting the neighbourhood to next Wednesday's meeting.
	Delaney overhears a conversation between Jack Jr. and a friend who discuss Mexican girls in a very unfriendly way.
	Kyra's first person to convince of the necessity of a wall is Delaney who does not like the idea of a seven foot wall in his back yard blocking his view of the landscape.
	Delaney confronts a Mexican who approaches the Cherrystones' house and grabs his arm.
	After Osbert's death Jack has asked Kyra to help convince the neighbourhood that they all need a wall around their development.
1	Kyra does not like going back to the Da Ros Place because she cannot forget the encounter with the two men.
	A neighbor approaches Delaney and tries to win his vote against the wall at the next meeting on Wednesday. Delaney thinks about the fights that would ensue with Kyra and Jack and hesitates to give his support.
	Three weeks later Kyra is back at the Da Ros Place still insecure because of the drifters. When she leaves the house she finds PINCHE PUTA sprayed on the back wall of the house.
	Delaney is sad because he is on his own and does not even have the dogs for company.

While-reading assignments part 2, chapter 7

Fill in the grid using an English-English and an English-German dictionary.

word	English definition	German
groceries p. 199, l. 12		
deprivation p. 199, l. 32		
garbled p. 200, l. 41		
pavement p. 201, l. 29		
to melt p. 202, l. 23		
bleak p. 202, l. 29		
trash p. 203, l. 37		
defeated p. 204, l. 1		
to scrape p. 205, l. 35		
grunt p. 206, l. 15		

While-reading assignments part 2, chapter 8

Finish the following sentences.

1. Out on a hike Delaney decides to go back home earlier than planned because ______________________________

2. Delaney almost does not open the door when the bell rings because ______________________________

3. Whereas Delaney has done nothing to stop the building of the wall and has not even gone to the decisive meeting Kyra ______________________________

4. Delaney accompanies Kyra to lock up the Da Ros Place every night because ______________________________

5. Delaney is amazed at the supermarket cashier because ______________________________

6. After their disastrous trip to Canoga Park América ______________________________

7. Señor Willis is ______________________________

8. On Thanksgiving Cándido goes to the supermarket to buy ______________________________

9. Two young men at the supermarket cashier give Cándido their free turkey because ______________________________

10. Cándido and América cannot enjoy roast turkey because ______________________________

Component 3

When Mexican dreams meet US reality

3.1 Delaney's worries

In diesem *Component* werden Vorschläge zur Erarbeitung des zweiten Teils des Romans gemacht. Es werden dabei drei Hauptschwerpunkte gesetzt: zum einen eine Beschränkung auf die Entwicklung der weißen Protagonisten, dann eine genaue Betrachtung der Zwischenfälle, die Weiße und Mexikaner gleichermaßen betreffen, und im dritten Teil eine Bearbeitung der Textstellen, die sich ausschließlich auf die Mexikaner beziehen. Diese Unterteilung lässt den Lehrkräften Spielraum zum Setzen eigener Schwerpunkte. Es empfiehlt sich, eine Mischung aus jedem der drei Teile zu wählen. Alles ausführlich zu behandeln, wird aus Zeitgründen kaum machbar sein. Darüber hinaus erscheint es sinnvoll, die Kapitel 1, 2, 3 und 6 ausführlich zu behandeln. Parallel dazu sollen die Schülerinnen und Schüler *part three* lesen und die ***Copies 23–30*** bearbeiten.

Zu Beginn der intensiven Arbeit an diesem Teil des Romans werden zunächst die ***Copies 14–20*** besprochen, um sicherzustellen, dass die Schülerinnen und Schüler den Inhalt von *part two* verstanden haben.

Solutions:

Copy 14

1. A Slim Jim is a tool used to break into cars.
2. According to Delaney the most annoying thing is his horrible laughter.
3. The American Way as defined in this part of the novel is buying something expensive and feeling good about it.
4. Kyra sees a dog locked in one of the cars on the parking lot although it is very hot.
5. She thinks that such a big group of Mexicans is bad for her business.
6. There are also snakes.
7. Her thoughts run along the lines of joy-riding teenagers, gardeners or illegal Mexicans.
8. At the restaurant Kyra felt safe and she realized that the white man who she was yelling at was impolite but basically harmless. The men at the villa are Mexicans, look at her in a hateful way, seem to be really dangerous and she is on her own.

Copy 15

1. Police officers: "What is a Mexican doing up here? I thought they only went to California to pick fruit. It is incredible that they now even invade our region."
2. The man: "Oh my God, what is he doing here? How did he come here? The poor guy looks awful."
3. Graciela: "The poor man – what rotten luck to come up here and then to lose your car and your friends. I hope he will be more successful in the south."
4. Resurreción: "Oh good, he will be here for Christmas. I wonder what gifts he will bring."
5. A woman: "Oh no – they will send us back, what bad luck. What can I tell my family? I haven't made enough money."
6. Al Lopez: "This is a good crew – I'm glad I found them. I think they'll enjoy some food and coke."

7. América: "I must never tell Cándido what has happened. It is too awful to talk about. I feel so ashamed."
8. Al Lopez: "I'm really sorry for this guy, but it is just too dangerous to employ illegal Mexicans. What if I am caught? And I do have people with papers, so why should I risk it?"

Copy 16

1. right	2. wrong	3. wrong	4. right	5. wrong
6. right	7. wrong	8. right	9. wrong	

2. Kyra uses her contacts to get rid of the labour exchange.
3. Kyra feels that there are just too many illegal immigrants.
5. Jim Shirley tells a horrible story about a neighbor who was raped in her home. He strongly supports the idea of a wall.
7. Dominick Flood must wear that device because he has embezzled money.
9. The coyote gets over the fence, robs Osbert and leaves with him into the canyon.

Copy 17

1. c	2. b	3. a	4. b	5. b
6. a	7. c	8. a	9. b	

Copy 18

4 – 10 – 6 – 3 – 9 – 2 – 1 – 8 – 5 – 7

Copy 19

word	English definition	German
groceries p. 199, l. 12	food and other goods sold at a supermarket	Lebensmittel
deprivation p. 199, l. 32	the fact of not having sth that you need like enough food, money or a home	Entbehrung
garbled p. 200, l. 41	told in a way that confuses the person listening	verworren
pavement p. 201, l. 29	surface of a road	Asphalt
to melt p. 202, l. 23	to become or make sth liquid as a result of heating	schmelzen
bleak p. 202, l. 29	exposed, empty, with no pleasant features	kahl, öde
trash p. 202, l. 37	things that you throw away because you no longer want or need them	Müll
defeated p. 204, l. 1	to be beaten in a war, competition or game	unterlegen
to scrape p. 205, l. 35	to remove sth from a surface by moving sth sharp and hard like a knife across it	etw. abkratzen
grunt p. 206, l. 15	short, low sound made by a person or animal	Grunzen

Copy 20

1. ... it is too hot and dusty to be outside.
2. ... he values his private writing time.
3. ... has aggressively supported the idea.
4. ... Kyra is too terrified to be out there on her own after the incident with the sprayed message.
5. ... they are offered a free turkey because they bought goods for more than $50.
6. ... is in a catatonic state and refuses to talk to Cándido.
7. ... a drunk old man who offers Cándido a well-paid job.
8. ... rice, canned tomatoes, milk and beer.
9. ... they have no use for it and do not even know how to cook it.
10. ... they set the canyon on fire when they try to roast the bird.

Nach der inhaltlichen Rekapitulation steigt man in die intensive Besprechung einzelner Kapitel ein. Zunächst werden die Schülerinnen und Schüler gefragt, was wohl der Titel *El Tenksgeevee* bedeuten soll. Mit Sicherheit kommen sie darauf, dass es sich um eine spanische Verballhornung des Begriffs *Thanksgiving* handelt. In einem Brainstorming wird abgefragt, was sie über diesen wichtigen amerikanischen Feiertag wissen.

What do you know about Thanksgiving?

- national holiday in the US and Canada
- celebrated on the fourth Thursday in November
- started in 1621 by William Bradford, who wanted to thank God for helping the settlers in their first difficult years in the new world
- remembering that Native Americans shared their food with the settlers and saved them
- traditional family dinner has a turkey at its centrepiece accompanied by stuffing, mashed potatoes, sweet corn and various fall vegetables; for dessert a pumpkin pie is always welcome
- typical decorations are carved pumpkins that are set outside the house
- ...

Im Anschluss an dieses Brainstorming wird die Frage gestellt, wofür die einzelnen Charaktere des Romans dankbar sein könnten. Dafür wird der Kurs in vier Gruppen geteilt, die auflisten, was Kyra, Delaney, Cándido und América nennen könnten, wenn gefragt, wofür sie an *Thanksgiving* dankbar sein werden. Die Ergebnisse dieser kurzen Gruppenarbeitsphase werden im Plenum besprochen und auf einer Folie oder an der Tafel festgehalten.

What could Kyra, Delaney, Cándido and América be thankful for that Thanksgiving?

Kyra	Delaney
• son and husband • good job – selling expensive houses • no financial worries • beautiful new home • good looks • ...	• financial independence • time for hikes • hobby is his job – writing articles • good second marriage • nice stepson • ...

América	Cándido
• has left desolate village in Mexico and made it to the US	• has found new girlfriend after his wife has left him
• has found good boyfriend	• has found jobs in the US
• is pregnant, looks forward to baby	• could leave Mexico
• can work when Cándido is injured	• can make money by working hard
• has found shelter in the canyon	• looks forward to his first baby
• ...	• ...

Nach der Präsentation der Ergebnisse wird der Fokus darauf gelegt, dass trotzdem einige ungünstige Ereignisse im Leben der Protagonisten eintreten. Als erstes wird da der Diebstahl von Delaneys Auto erwähnt werden. Kyra ist glücklos beim Versuch den Da Ros Place zu verkaufen und fühlt sich sogar durch die Anwesenheit der beiden jungen hispanischen Männer bedroht. América wird vergewaltigt und Cándido wird verprügelt und ausgeraubt; beide befinden sich ohne Geld und Arbeit in einer hoffnungslosen Situation.

Als Hausaufgabe sollen die Schülerinnen und Schüler in einem Text herausarbeiten, welche Wirkung der Diebstahl und die Reaktion seiner Mitmenschen auf Delaney haben.

What effect does the theft of his car have on Delaney? How do others react to the crime? (part two, chapter 1)

Delaney is disappointed because everybody seems to calmly accept the fact that someone stole his car. The fact that many cars are stolen is no comfort to him. The frequent repetition of the phrase "happens all the time" (four times in the first three paragraphs of this chapter) and the police's "enthusiasm of the walking dead" (p. 129) when taking the report demonstrate just how very normal an incident like this is. It is regarded as inevitable as "tax, winter floods and mudslides" (p. 129) (The mentioning of "mudslide" here is also a foreshadowing of the end of the novel.) Kenny Grissom's remark that he does not blame it all on the Mexicans, but also on "Salvadorians, Iranians, Russians, Vietnamese" (p. 129) shows that he does not think at all that a white American could possibly have stolen the car. In this respect he is just as racist in his attitude as Jack Jardine who uses this crime to influence Delaney further and to change his attitude from sympathetic to racist. He calls people like Delaney "bleeding hearts" (p. 129) who invite all the world to come to the USA. He compares the situation in Arroyo Blanco with a war: "We're under siege here – and there's going to be a blacklash" (p. 129). (The backlash possibly being a foreshadowing of the scene where Delaney and his upper-middle-class neighbours turn into a nasty mob.)
A first consequence of all this talk is that Delaney feels somewhat reluctant to hand his new car over to the young Hispanic who is the valet parking attendant of the Indian restaurant where he wants to meet Kyra for lunch.

Zu Beginn der nächsten Stunde wird der Kurs in Kleingruppen von je vier Schülerinnen und Schülern eingeteilt, die sich ihre Texte gegenseitig vorlesen, eine Fehlerkorrektur vornehmen und dann die beste Hausaufgabe auswählen. Je nach Kursgröße kann man dann in je drei Gruppen den wiederum besten Text auswählen lassen, sodass zum Schluss die besten beiden Hausaufgaben im Plenum vorgetragen werden.

Im Anschluss an diese Phase werden zwei weitere Aspekte im Unterrichtsgespräch besprochen.

What can you say about Kenny Grissom's views on Mexicans/illegal immigrants? (part two, chapter 1)

- seems to be happy about many car thefts – good for business
- knows a lot about exact proceedings of these thefts (who orders, who sells ...)
- makes fun of ignorant woman from Guatemala
- ➡ typical car dealer, viewing everything from the businessman's point of view

Why does Delaney have the feeling of "losing control" (p. 130) and "as if his luck had turned bad" (p. 131)?

Delaney's comfortable life has been disturbed by his inner conflict about how to feel about the Mexicans. Also the tragic losses of Sacheverell and his car have shaken him. It seems as if the American way is no longer working for him. "Buy something. Feel good. But he didn't feel good, not at all. He felt like a victim." (p. 132) Of course, he is a victim, after all his car has been stolen.
An example of his loss of control is that he cannot remember his new license plate number. He used to have personalised number plates, namely PILGRIM, and the fact that he does without these shows that he has already given up some of his identity as Pilgrim to Topanga Creek, living in harmony with society and nature.

Ein Ziel bei der Bearbeitung eines Romans ist die stilistische Analyse von Textstellen. Um den Schülerinnen und Schülern dabei Hilfestellungen zu geben, findet sich hier ein zweiseitiges *Worksheet* mit den in *The Tortilla Curtain* häufig vorkommenden stilistischen Mitteln. Die ausgewählte Textstelle, *part two, chapter 1* bietet sich besonders für ein solches Unterfangen an, da T. C. Boyle hier konzentriert Stilmittel einsetzt, um dem Leser Delaneys sich allmählich wandelnde Einstellung deutlich zu machen. Dabei werden sowohl komische als auch ernsthafte Effekte erzielt. Man sollte zunächst gemeinsam mit den Schülerinnen und Schülern die aufgelisteten Stilmittel besprechen, sie im Textzusammenhang nachlesen und ihren jeweiligen Effekt untersuchen. Daraufhin können die beiden *Assignments* entweder als Partnerarbeit oder als Hausaufgabe gestellt werden.

Copy 21 wird zunächst im Kurs verteilt, die aufgelisteten Stilmittel werden gemeinsam besprochen, die Beispiele werden im Textzusammenhang gelesen und ihr jeweiliger Effekt wird besprochen. Danach werden die Schülerinnen und Schüler aufgefordert, in Partnerarbeit die Aufgabe auf ***Copy 21*** zu bearbeiten, wobei der Text in vier Abschnitte aufgeteilt wird, auf die sich gleich viele Paare konzentrieren sollen. Die Textabschnitte werden auf Folie kopiert und dann von einzelnen Paaren beschriftet und der Effekt der Stilmittel erläutert.

Hier ein kurzer Erwartungshorizont für die Aufgabe auf *Copy 21*:

anaphora
p. 152 ll. 2 ff. "Was it worth dying for this? ... it wasn't worth it. ... it wasn't worth it."
p. 152, ll. 31 f. "He watched the trees ... He watched the groundsquirrels, the birds, watched light ..."

alliteration
p. 151, l. 1 "... Spanish speaking immigration ..."
p. 151, l. 45 "... ragged roaring ..."

climactic sentence structure
p. 150, l. 36 "... the doors locked, the windows barred, all their possessions – left behind."

exaggeration
p. 152, l. 14 "... then the sound of all the glass in the world shattering."

flashback
die gesamte Szene ist Teil eines Flashbacks.

Interior monologue
p. 151, ll. 17 f. "Run! Run now while ..."

metaphor
p. 150, l. 35 "... puke-green buses ..."
p. 151, ll. 9 – 11 "... and the Mexicans ... rooted to the pavement ..."
p. 151, l. 33 "... the torrent of headlights."
p. 151, l. 45 "... ragged roaring whine of engines ..."
p. 152, l. 2 "... sirens tore at the air ..."
p. 152, ll. 21 – 23 "... while the apocalypse of twisted metal and skating cars blasted the world around him till even the traffic across the divider was stopped dead in horror."
p. 152, l. 24 "... walked on melting legs ..."

paratactical sentence structure
p. 150, l. 44 "It was cold. A woman was crying softly beside him; a man argued with ..."

rhetorical question
p. 152, l. 2 "Was it worth dying for this?"

simile
p. 152, l. 17 "The first boy went down like a piston ..."

Kapitel 5 im zweiten Teil des Romans fällt insofern aus dem Rahmen, als es nicht die Geschichte weitererzählt sondern der Leser eine Kostprobe von Delaneys Tätigkeit als Pilgrim bekommt. In diesem Artikel beschäftigt er sich mit der Ausbreitung der Kojoten, die als Kulturfolger immer näher an die Behausungen der Menschen heranrücken. Delaney als Hundebesitzer muss schmerzhaft erfahren, wie geschickt diese Tiere ihren Vorteil sehen und gnadenlos ihre Beute reißen.
Dieses Kapitel handelt vordergründig von Kojoten, allerdings wird schnell deutlich, dass viele Formulierungen auch auf die immer stärker ins Land drängenden illegalen Einwanderer aus Mexiko bezogen werden können. Diese Textstellen sollen von den Schülerinnen und Schülern in Partnerarbeit identifiziert und erläutert werden. Dabei wird die Kenntnis des gesamten bis jetzt gelesenen Textes vorausgesetzt. Eine Tabelle wird an der Tafel skizziert und soll von den Schülerinnen und Schülern ausgefüllt werden.

Read chapter 5 again and identify which statements refer to coyotes. In how far can they also be referred to illegal Mexican immigrants? Make a grid.

page	coyotes	Mexicans
184 l. 18	The coyote has been much on my mind.	Delaney is preoccupied with the topic ever since he has hit Cándido and has started to suspect that a Mexican has stolen his car.
...		

Lösungsvorschlag:

page	coyotes	Mexicans
184 l. 36	And then, no doubt to the very day, the coyote will be back.	As Cándido himself says being deported is no big deal because you will be back in no time. (Chapter 2, p. 152, l. 3)
184 l. 40 f.	... call the Los Angeles County Animal Control Department, which traps and euthanizes about 100 coyotes a year.	An equivalent to this department is La Migra.
185 l. 4	... the coyote roamed these hills long before Homo sapiens made his first shaggy appearance...	Up to the Texas annexation in 1845 today's California was Mexican territory.
185 l. 6 f.	... this author has begun to feel that some sort of control must be applied...	Not only has Delaney lost another little dog to a coyote, he also has the feeling that he is losing his inner calm because of the increasing amount of Hispanic immigrants.
185 l. 36 f.	... they actually donate their kitchen scraps to his well-being.	Americans give Mexicans the lowest possible jobs so that they can survive, e. g. scrubbing Buddhas or clearing construction sites.
186 l. 25 f.	We cannot eradicate the coyote, nor can we fence him out ...	The surge of illegal immigrants coming into the country cannot be stopped, not even by a border that is getting ever more protected by border control agencies like La Migra.
186 l. 33 f.	The coyote is not to blame – he is only trying to survive, to make a living ...	You cannot blame people for coming to the US to fulfil their American dream.
186 l. 41 f.	The coyotes keep coming ... They are cunning, versatile, hungry and unstoppable.	As the example of Cándido shows not even bad luck will deter Mexicans from trying their luck time and again.

Delaney, der sich für einen liberalen Menschen gehalten hat, muss feststellen, dass sich seine Haltung den Mitmenschen aus Mexiko gegenüber ändert. Besonders deutlich wird das in Kapitel 6, wo die Forderung, eine Mauer um *Arroyo Blanco* zu ziehen, ernsthaft in Erwägung gezogen wird. Nach dem Vorfall mit Osbert ist vor allem Kyra sehr für eine solche Befestigung ihrer Wohnanlage.
Die Schülerinnen und Schüler sollen als Hausaufgabe die entsprechenden Textstellen markieren und einen kurzen zusammenfassenden Text schreiben.

Read chapter 6 and mark all the statements that refer to Delaney's attitude towards a wall around Arroyo Blanco and the presence of illegal immigrants. Then write a short text working out the development of Delany's position.

- vehement opposition "But that's crazy" (p. 190)
- clear anti-racist attitude in discussion (p. 190)
- tolerance towards Mexicans
- worried about Jordan's future in Arroyo Blanco
- doubts about his own attitudes "... his mind gone numb with ambivalence" (p. 196)
- clear racist behaviour when personally confronted with Mexican (pp. 197/198)

Nach der Erarbeitung dieses Schwerpunktes kann jetzt am nächsten Aspekt, dem Zusammentreffen von Weißen und Mexikanern, weitergearbeitet werden.

3.2 When Whites and Mexicans meet

Die folgende Aufgabe eignet sich zur Bearbeitung in Partnerarbeit, die Ergebnisse können stichwortartig an der Tafel festgehalten werden.

How do the Mossbachers establish contact with the Mexicans in part two, chapter 1?

- There is indirect contact when Kenny Grissom tells Delaney that rich Mexicans order cars to be stolen by their countrymen in California (pp. 128 – 129).
- Delaney hands his new car to the parking valet who is a Latino, Delaney feels a moment of racist resentment at that encounter (p. 130).
- The fear of another Mexican gang stealing his new car makes Delaney sit in the bushes, not daring to leave his car alone in the wilderness, watching it instead of going on a hike (p. 137).
- Kyra becomes aware of how many Mexicans are hanging around Ventura Boulevard just a couple of blocks away from her business area and she decides to do something about it (p. 138 f.). Ironically, the Mexicans were at first good for her business because they made rich white people want to leave Los Angeles' inner city areas.
- When Kyra stops to buy something at a small supermarket she feels all the Mexican men's eyes on her, a young man offers himself as a cheap worker to her (p. 138 f.).
- Kyra decides to have a higher fence because of what has happened to Sacheverell; when she watches the Mexicans who work for her contractor, Al Lopez (obviously also an immigrant from south of the border), she recognises Cándido as the man who was hit by Delaney's car (p. 140 f.).
- Later, when she is closing down the Da Ros place she notices a shopping cart in the bush; she checks the area and meets two Mexicans, who should not be there. It seems as if they are the same men who raped América earlier. Kyra is afraid of them, but manages to scare them away (pp. 144 – 145).

Nachdem die Schülerinnen und Schüler die Beziehungen von Weißen und Mexikanern zu Beginn des zweiten Teils untersucht haben, können sie nun detailliert auf die unterschiedlichen Frauenrollen in den beiden Kulturen anhand von América und Kyra eingehen.
Dazu wird der Kurs in zwei Hälften geteilt, die sich mit je einem der beiden weiblichen Charaktere beschäftigen. In einer *Hot Seat*-Phase sollen beide Frauen genauer betrachtet werden. Dazu wird im Kurs ***Copy 22*** verteilt, das es den Schülerinnen und Schülern ermöglicht, anhand von 20 Fragen ihren Charakter näher kennenzulernen. Wenn nach einer Erarbeitungsphase von 15 – 20 Minuten die Antworten formuliert sind, wird je eine Schülerin ausgewählt, die auf dem *Hot Seat* Platz nimmt und Auskunft über ihren Charakter erteilt. Danach wird eine Liste von Fragen an Kyra bzw. América ausgearbeitet, die diesem Charakter gestellt werden sollen. Auch diese Phase wird 15 – 20 Minuten dauern. (vgl. Method Guide 1 – Methoden für den Englischunterricht Klasse 5 – 13, Paderborn: Schöningh 2016, S. 131)
Nachdem eine der Schülerinnen in der Mitte des Raumes auf dem *Hot Seat* Platz genommen hat, beginnt die Fragerunde. Wenn alles Wichtige genannt ist, nimmt eine andere Schülerin Platz, um Auskunft über die andere der beiden Frauen zu erteilen. Auf diese Weise erarbeiten die Schülerinnen und Schüler ein Charakterbild der beiden wichtigen Figuren. Als Hausaufgabe werden die Ergebnisse der Stunde anhand der folgenden Leitfrage zusammengefasst.

América and Kyra represent two totally different types of women. Comment on the two different roles as women that América and Kyra assume.

América	Kyra
in eternal fear of being caught by La Migra, sometimes hit and abused by husband (p. 159)	assertive, courageous businesswoman, violently confronts a man who does not treat his pet correctly in her opinion (p. 134)
not daring to defend herself when sexually abused (grabs, rape)	when passing a group of Mexicans she is in control (p. 140)
feels uneasy and menaced when she is near Mexican men (p. 54)	although fearful she confronts the two trespassers (p. 144)
➡ submissive, fearful and completely subject to her hushband's will	➡ self-assertive, independent woman fighting for her rights

Für die nächste Erarbeitung, die sich mit dem Verhältnis der illegalen Einwanderer zu der Einwanderungsbehörde *La Migra* beschäftigt, wird der Kurs in drei Gruppen geteilt, die sich mit je einer Aufgabenstellung beschäftigen und die Ergebnisse im Plenum vorstellen. Die Textstelle ist von der Stilmittelanalyse her den Schülerinnen und Schülern vertraut und kann nun inhaltlich genauer untersucht werden.
Nach dem Vorlesen der Seiten 150–152 können die Schülerinnen und Schüler in Gruppen- oder Partnerarbeit und im anschließenden Unterrichtsgespräch untersuchen, wie T.C. Boyle sprachlich Cándidos Verachtung für Angehörige dieser Behörde zum Ausdruck bringt, obwohl ein eigentlicher Grund zum Hass nicht gegeben ist. Die Vermutung liegt nahe, dass er seine eigenen Schuldgefühle durch Hass auf *La Migra* betäuben möchte.

How does Cándido describe members of La Migra? (Chapter 2)

The overall impression of the Border Patrol tends to be very negative. The reader sees the immigration officers only through the eyes of this illegal immigrant whose one and only concern is how to get past them. He uses derogatory language:

- puke-green buses (p. 150, l. 35)
- fat-faced overfed pendejo (p. 151, l. 18)
- green-eyed bitch (p. 151, l. 20)
- macho corps of the immigration (p. 151, l. 23)
- their faces contorted and ugly with their shouts and threats (p. 151, ll. 8–9)

Cándido seems to hate La Migra so much that even faced by the greatest danger, he does not want to give himself up to them. "Something uncoiled inside of him ... like a cornered rabbit leaping from a cliff to avoid the dogs." (p. 152, ll. 9–11) Nevertheless, he knows all the time that nothing worse will happen than being sent home and having to return a couple of days later.

How do the immigration agents treat the illegal immigrants they catch? (chapter 2)

Cándido's own knowledge of what is likely to happen if they get arrested by the Border Patrol belies his negative utterances. While in some countries they would face severe beatings, could be killed or sentenced to many years in detention camps or prisons, the American immigration agents will merely transport them back to or beyond the border (p. 152). From there, the Mexicans can attempt any number of new crossings until they succeed.

What makes Cándido feel that he would never forgive himself "for what happened next"? (chapter 2, p. 152, l. 5)

Reflecting on the fatal accidents, he is aware that only he knew the real risks that the whole situation along the freeway posed. He thinks he should have known that the freeway was much more dangerous than the immigration agents behind them. Running across the freeway meant risking their lives, but being picked up by La Migra only meant that they could be back "in a day ... a week" (p. 152, ll. 3 f.).
It was also his responsibility to take care of the two young men not only because of his age, but also because of his greater experience on North Américan soil. He should have put the welfare of the group above his own. His hate of La Migra was so strong that he followed his self-destructive impulse, "something uncoiled inside of him" (p. 152, l. 9).

Nach Abschluss der intensiven Besprechung dieser Episode bietet sich eine *creative writing*-Aufgabe als Hausaufgabe an. Dabei sollen die Schülerinnen und Schüler darauf achten, die Fakten richtig wiederzugeben und eine eigene Stellungnahme bzw. eigene Gefühle mit einzubringen.

You are a reporter for an American newspaper. By chance, you have seen the two attempts made by Cándido and his two companions at escaping the immigration officers. Write an article about what you have witnessed.
OR
You are one of the officers involved in this incident. At the police station you tell your colleagues about it.

Als Alternative bietet sich eine Übung im Schreiben von *comments* an. Wiederum gibt es die Möglichkeit, unter zwei Themen zu wählen.

In 1994 a high fence was added to the central divide between the northbound and southbound lanes of the San Diego Freeway as one approaches the INS (Immigration and Naturalization Service) checkpoint at San Onofre from the south. What does this development tell you about the immigration situation in Southern California? Write a personal comment.
OR
It is estimated that three to four million illegal immigrants currently live in California. About 300,000 to 500,000 are believed to cross the 2,500 mile US-Mexican border every year. How are these figures likely to influence readers views of Cándido's escape? (Personal comment)

Selbstverständlich eignen sich diese Aufgaben auch hervorragend für Klausuren. In der folgenden Stunde werden die Ergebnisse der Hausaufgabe besprochen. Die Schüler können jetzt die im Kapitel 2 geschilderten geographischen Gegebenheiten visuell umsetzen, indem sie ein großformatiges Bild erstellen. Ein gelungenes Bild wird dann gemeinsam ausgesucht und der Romancollage hinzugefügt (vgl. Ausführungen zu *Component 1*, S. 12).

In Kapitel 3 kommt es erneut zu einem Treffen einiger Mitglieder der *Arroyo Blanco community*. Die Seiten 162 – 166 sollten die Schülerinnen und Schüler laut mit verteilten Rollen lesen, danach kann mit der arbeitsteiligen Gruppenarbeit begonnen werden, bei der einzelne Positionen herausgearbeitet werden. Nach Erstellen des Tafelbildes wird eine Diskussion in der Klasse geführt.

At the community's second meeting various opinions are voiced by the inhabitants. Identify the speakers and their statements, then have a similar discussion in class. (chapter 3)
For your own discussion think of liberal arguments that Delaney might have had at the beginning of this novel and have one group be a supporter of such liberal humanist ideas.

Jim Shirley
- suggests that phone numbers should not be listed any more, he gives two examples of tricks that are used by Mexican burglars
- ➡ introduction of more security measures
- dwells on the details of a particularly heavy assault on a resident
- ➡ purpose of shocking the listeners and getting their support for more security

Jack Jardine
- suggests that the area should be walled in by pointing out the weaknesses of a gate
- ➡ introduction of even stronger security measures

Dominick Flood
- reports that the labour exchange will be closed down because of his intervention
- ➡ emphasis on strong measures to drive Mexicans away

Jack Cherrystone
- project of labour exchange was wrong from the start
- high unemployment rate in Los Angeles
- a future reduction in the crime rate
- too many Mexicans everywhere
- ➡ emphasis on strong measures to drive Mexicans away

Delaney
- the US is a nation of immigrants – every American has roots in a foreign country
- Mexicans have every right to enter the country
- all men are created equal
- cheap labour is needed to keep prices for farm goods low
- immigrants are not automatically criminals
- white people can be criminals, too
- ...

Nach der Durchführung der Diskussion, an der fünf Schülerinnen oder Schüler aktiv teilnehmen, wird gemeinsam evaluiert, wie effektiv die Teilnehmer argumentiert haben. Im Anschluss daran bespricht man, wie die Schülerinnen und Schüler sich fühlen würden, wenn sie in einem solch gesicherten Wohnkomplex leben müssten.

Imagine you lived in a gated community as the inhabitants of Arroyo Blanco plan to create. What would you like? What would you not find agreeable?

Possible answers:

Pros	Cons
• life would be safer • people would know each other better • community meetings strengthen the ties in the neighbourhood • ...	• you would feel like a criminal living behind bars • it would be more difficult to invite friends • too much control between neighbours • ....

Als Hausaufgabe soll Kapitel 8 (part two) noch einmal gelesen werden und die beiden *community meetings*, die der Leser verfolgt hat, sollen in einem kurzen Text miteinander verglichen werden.

Work out the differences between the first (pp. 41ff.) and the second (pp. 164ff.) meeting.

Whereas in the first meeting some residents still point out the freedom of every individual and resent any kind of elitist behaviour or discrimination of some groups, the anti-Mexican tendency is voiced much more strongly and the measures to be taken are much more vehement in the second meeting. Nobody mentions the desperate situation of the Mexicans. It is interesting to note that the person who finally takes the decisive steps in uprooting the labour exchange is somebody who has been sentenced himself. His offence was mishandling funds, in other words he is a thief, even though he seems to be socially accepted.
At the second meeting Delaney does not make any comment except an irritated remark in which he anticipates the plan that they all have: a wall around the estate. Having been confronted with it, Delaney is silent. There is only one other occasion when he says something, that is when the others slightly make fun of him because of his appearance during the last meeting when speaking out against feeding the wildlife.
Summing up, the tone of the second meeting is much more aggressive and assertive than that of the first one. The issue is only looked at from one side except for Delaney's little outburst.

Vor der Besprechung der Hausaufgabe wird stichwortartig an der Tafel festgehalten, welche Hauptunterschiede es zwischen den beiden Versammlungen gibt. Danach lesen einzelne Schülerinnen und Schüler ihre Texte vor und der Kurs bewertet, ob die Aufgabe umfassend gelöst wurde.
Im Anschluss daran wird in Partnerarbeit herausgearbeitet, wie die beiden Paare auf verschiedene Lebensmittel reagieren und wie unterschiedlich die Menschen auf die verschenkten Truthähne an der Supermarktkasse reagieren. Dazu wird die Aufgabenstellung an die Tafel geschrieben oder per Overheadfolie projiziert. Die Antworten werden in kurzen mündlichen Vorträgen präsentiert.

Show how the mood of the couples in influenced by the exposure to special foods (part two, chapter 8).

Delaney and Kyra	Cándido and América
they have an argument about the necessity of the wall and the responsibility of the Da Ros place	América suffers from a nervous breakdown and is completely shattered
the superabundant variety of the goods in the supermarket makes Delaney feel tender towards Kyra	The free gift of the turkey raises Cándido's spirits enormously and the prospect of eating improves América's mental state
➡ they are reconciled	➡ she smiles again

We witness the giving away of two turkeys at the supermarket. What are the differences? (part two, chapter 8)

When Kyra and Delaney get their turkey, a new trait of Kyra's is revealed. She is greedy for the turkey although the Mossbachers have already got one. She cuts Delaney short when he starts to refuse the gift. By doing that she confirms Cándido's prejudice about the greedy whites who, although living in the best circumstances, still want more and more.
When Cándido is offered the turkey by the two men who are in line in front of him, he does not even realize what they are doing. He is really thankful and feels very lucky for a change.

3.3 The Mexicans' desperate struggle for happiness

Im dritten Teil dieses *Components* finden sich Anregungen zur Diskussion von Problemen, die die Lebensumstände von Cándido und América betreffen. Als Einstieg in ein Unterrichtsgespräch über deren Situation könnte die Frage dienen, ob die Schülerinnen und Schüler sich in ihre Lage versetzen können. Obwohl dies vermutlich verneint werden muss, können in einem Tafelbild stichwortartig einzelne Lebensbedingungen, die in *part one* beschrieben wurden, festgehalten werden. Es darf spekuliert werden, wie sich die Lebensverhältnisse der beiden weiter entwickeln könnten (vgl. Diskussion zum Titel von *part two, El Tenksgeevee*).

Falls bereits über die unterschiedlichen Rollen von Frauen in diesem Roman gesprochen wurde, erübrigt sich ggf. die nachfolgende Frage, falls nicht, ergibt sich aus dieser Frage vermutlich ein lebhaftes Gespräch über Frauenrollen, bzw. Gewalt in der Familie.

Why does Cándido hit his wife (part two, chapter 2)?

He hits América because she is the person in his life who is even weaker and less successful than he is. He must find a way of relief for his frustration and wants to feel superior to someone.

Bezugnehmend auf die Bearbeitung wesentlicher Fragen des vorangegangenen Teils kann hier noch einmal auf die dort erarbeiteten Ergebnisse zurückgegriffen werden und Cándidos und Américas unterschiedliche Reaktionen auf die Nachricht, dass der *Labour Exchange* geschlossen wurde, untersucht werden. Es bietet sich hier eine kleine Gruppenarbeit an; eine Gruppe untersucht Cándidos Reaktion, eine andere Américas. In der anschließenden Diskussion wird ein Tafelbild erstellt.

Die beiden jetzt folgenden Aufgaben bieten sich auch als Klausuraufgaben an. Falls die stilistischen Mittel in den vorhergehenden Aufgaben besprochen wurden, kann auch noch die anschließende Arbeitsanweisung als Klausuraufgabe herangezogen werden.

Why is Cándido so shocked when he finds out that the labour exchange is closed? (part two, chapter 4)

Cándido is shocked because he wants to protect América from the dangerous life in the street. He has planned to save all the money they need and then move to an apartment directly from the canyon. He knows life in the cities from his previous stays in the US.
He feels that they have been quite close to success and is angry that now they will have to leave the canyon. He momentarily thinks of committing suicide: "Why not kill himself now and get it all over with?" (p. 174) and "Or should he just die on the spot ..." (p. 175). He compares Mexico, the country to which he cannot return, to the USA where obviously he cannot survive either. He is mad about the fact that he is refused the right to work.

Why is América quite happy when she hears the news? (part two, chapter 4)

América is bored by her dull life alone in the canyon. She also wants to have a bath and a bed since she is troubled by her pregnancy. She is afraid of the people in the canyon and she is constantly reminded of the rape. She dreams of a much better life in the city.

Read pp. 174 f. again and compare the information given about Mexico and the USA.

Mexico	USA
• 40 % unemployment	• right to riches of the world
• 1 million people a year entering the work force	• white faces, high heels, business suits, greedy eyes, ravenous mouths
• only rich people have got enough to eat	• glass palaces
• people living in extreme poverty	• the value of exercise equipment alone is enough to feed a Third World country
	• even the poorest have got two cars

Sum up the incidents that lead to América's and Cándido's further defeat and their reactions to them. Then try to identify some of the stylistic devices T. C. Boyle uses to emphasise their desperate situation.

1. Several hours América waits for Cándido to come back. However, he does not show up.
   ➡ she is worried and approached by insinuating men (p. 202)
2. Cándido tells her that he has been robbed.
   ➡ all their hopes for the future are shattered (p. 202)

3. Cándido rummages in the trash to find something to eat.
   ➡ América is completely disgusted and refuses to take anything (p. 206)

ad 1)
América's anxiety is reflected by the many questions which she is asking herself:
"... and where was he?" (p. 201)
"... what if he'd had an accident? What if he was hurt? What if La Migra had snatched him? ... What if Cándido never came back, what if he'd died of a heart attack or got hit by another car? What then?" (p. 201)
"And where was Cándido? Where was the room he'd promised her, the bed, the shower?" (pp. 201 – 202)

This stylistic device of repeated questions emphasises América's fear and insecurity. She is, after all, a girl who is very young and inexperienced.

ad 2) and 3)
Metaphors and similes are used to show their defeat:
"... his face a flag of blood, his pantlegs flapping like ragged banners" (p. 204)
"... his shoulders squared up like a fighting cock's, his eyes eating up the street" (p. 204)
➡ He is compared to a fighting cock that cannot decide for himself but is pulled by invisible strings. He has to fight to survive, he is also ravenously hungry.
"... like a hermit crab emerging from its shell" (p. 206)
➡ In the same way as the only possession of the hermit crab is the shell, Cándido's only access to survival or food is the trash bin.

Um die Schülerinnen und Schüler auch emotional an die Problematik heranzuführen, kann man eine Diskussion zum Thema Eigenverantwortung mit ihnen über die nächste Frage anregen. Dabei könnten eigene Erfahrungen der Schülerinnen und Schüler mit eingebracht werden.

Cándido thinks that again his "stinking bad luck" (p. 203) has struck. Do you agree? (part two, chapter 7)

There are two ways of seeing this: either the students agree that it is just his tough luck or they find arguments for Cándido's own fault in his predicament, e.g. how could he have brought a young girl to the US, why is he so stupid and careless? They could report personal experiences with situations where they thought it was their tough luck that foiled their success or on the other hand situations where they realized that they had made mistakes.

Da die Frage des *point of view* bereits in *Component 1, **Copy 3*** behandelt wurde, bietet es sich an, eine erneute Aufgabe zu dem Thema zu stellen, um den Schülerinnen und Schülern anhand eines weiteren Beispiels deutlich zu machen, dass der *point of view* einen beträchtlichen Einfluss auf den Stil und die Wirkung eines Romans hat. Am Beispiel des Kapitels 7 (part two) kann man besonders gut zeigen, wie die Erzählperspektive die Emotionen der Leser wecken und ein direktes Mitfühlen mit den Protagonisten ermöglichen kann.

Part two, chapter 7 is mainly told from América's point of view, Cándido's thoughts are only presented to a very limited extent. What effect does this have on the reader?

The reader is told a lot about América's anxiety while waiting for Cándido as well as about her feelings about being in the US in general: "You got streets and bums and burning pee." (p. 202)
América's reaction to the news of having lost everything comes out very clearly; her shattered hopes are voiced and she even wants to die.

When Cándido rummages in the trash América's complete horror and outrage is voiced, she even points to the greater respectability of her family than Cándido's in her despair (p. 206). This is also a scene where T. C. Boyle shows his talent for irony. If the perspective was on Cándido, América's reactions and thoughts could never have been presented to the reader so clearly. Her disgust, outrage and despair become apparent and genuine.

Write down an interior monologue (see: *Copy 21*) for Cándido on his way back to América after having been mugged.

Falls man nicht allzu ausführlich auf die vorherigen Fragen eingehen möchte, bietet sich als Abschluss der Bearbeitung des zweiten Teils eine Rückschau auf die Träume der beiden und ihre reale Situation an.

What are the Mexicans' dreams and which nightmares do they have to endure?

dreams	**nightmares**
car, apartment (p. 158)	money stolen/América suffers as a result of rape
América dreams of city with shops, toilets, showers (p. 176).	dog-eat-dog world (p. 158, l. 11)
motel room for one night with shower and TV (p. 177)	no work for Cándido because illegal immigrant
América falls into trance when she is looking at a furniture store (p. 180)	they eat little birds (p. 171)
regular work with Señor Willis (p. 216)	closing down of labour exchange live on streets temptation to steal, humiliation at being given alms (p. 175 f.) realisation: no work in the city (p. 182) Cándido ripped off in the city (p. 202) eating from trash cans (p. 206) canyon on fire (p. 221)

Notizen:

Stylistic Devices

This is a list of stylistic devices that T. C. Boyle uses quite frequently in *The Tortilla Curtain*:

1. **anaphora**
   A word or phrase is repeated at the beginning of each of two or more successive clauses, sentences or paragraphs.
   p. 129: "Jack, ever calm, ever prepared, ever cynical ..."

2. **alliteration**
   Repetition of similar sounds in a sequence of associated words.
   p. 150: "all their poor possessions";
   p. 151: "It was the Mexican way: acquiesce, accept."

3. **climactic sentence structure**
   A series of words or ideas in an ascending order of significance or intensity.
   p. 132: "... he felt good about it, good about himself, the future of the country, the state of the world."

4. **exaggeration**
   An exaggeration makes sth. seem more important, better or worse than it is.
   p. 129: "when all you bleeding hearts want to invite the whole world in here."

5. **flashback**
   Interruption of the account of sth in order to portray an incident or a scene from the past.
   pp. 146 – 152: Cándido thinks about his first stay in the canyon six years ago.

6. **interior monologue**
   Author's technique that reproduces the flow of thoughts just as it occurs in a character's mind.
   p. 143: Kyra on her way to an appointment.

7. **irony**
   Humorous use of words to express a meaning other than the one literally conveyed by the words.
   p. 129: story about the woman from Guatemala who took the advertisement "we don't refuse credit" too literally.

8. **metaphor**
   The transference of a term from the object it ordinarily designates to an object it may designate only by implicit comparison or analogy.
   p. 128: Slim Jim as a name for breaking into cars.

9. **paratactical sentence structure**
   The joining together of clauses without the use of conjunctions.
   p. 129: "And now Kenny Grissom. Business as usual. A shoulder shrug, a wink of commiseration, the naked joy of moving product."

10. **rhetorical question**
    A question to which no answer is expected.
    p. 129: "Where do you think they sleep? What do you think they eat?"

11. **sarcasm**
    Apparent praise for dispraise.
    p. 129: "... enthusiasm of the walking dead."

12. **simile**
    Two unlike things are compared, indicated by a marker such as "like" or "as".
    p. 129: "It was like a tax, like winter floods and mudslides."

Read closely part two, chapter 2, p. 150, l. 29 ("And then the roof fell in ...") to p. 152, l. 34 (" and went home to Resurrección"). Find as many stylistic devices as you can and explain the intended effect.

Hot Seat

Task 1

Tune into your character. Try to get a feel for this woman. Look at these questions and find answers based on what you have read about her. If the information is not given, you will have to guess. Your classmates will ask you all kinds of things about yourself so be prepared.

1. What is your name/age?
2. Describe where you live.
3. What do you look like? How do you dress?
4. How do you move?
5. What typical gestures or facial expressions have you got?
6. What is your relationship to your parents like?
7. What is your social background?
8. Describe a typical day in your life.
9. How would you characterize yourself?
10. What are your greatest strengths?
11. What are your greatest weaknesses?
12. What are you afraid of?
13. What is especially important to you?
14. What values do you have?
15. What do you despise?
16. What is your main goal in life?
17. What was your biggest mistake recently?
18. What was your best/worst decision recently?
19. What are your greatest influences at present?
20. What was your greatest achievement recently?

Task 2

Prepare questions for the other group's character. Where would you like to find out more?
Ideas for questions:

- Could you tell us where/when/what/who/how ...?
- Could you explain why you ...?
- Could you tell us how you managed to ...?
- Why did/didn't you ...?
- What made you ...?
- What led you to ...?
- What happened when/after ...?
- How did you feel when ...?
- What were you thinking when ...?
- If you could choose again, would you ...?

While-reading assignments part III, chapter 1

Read part III, chapter 1, on pages 224 – 233.
Find 10 words from this chapter in this grid and insert the correct words in the following sentences. (↓↑↔↖↗↘↙)

	A	B	C	D	E	F	G	H	I	J	K	L	M	N	O
1	d	t	z	u	i	o	p	l	j	m	n	b	v	d	e
2	q	e	w	s	d	f	h	g	j	k	y	g	d	e	n
3	U	n	t	t	s	d	o	w	a	p	l	n	m	p	u
4	r	t	e	r	s	d	b	b	n	o	l	a	q	v	W
5	f	g	s	h	i	e	s	t	c	o	n	v	e	r	t
6	w	x	t	c	v	t	c	h	u	z	i	s	m	l	p
7	r	e	i	x	y	t	u	y	v	c	t	g	h	l	i
8	q	w	m	a	s	e	r	s	c	i	v	b	n	n	m
9	t	z	o	s	d	r	e	v	g	z	u	i	c	m	l
10	a	x	n	c	f	f	j	i	k	l	i	u	l	p	x
11	w	e	y	b	v	c	a	m	n	k	b	l	o	u	c
12	r	t	h	z	u	l	i	o	p	u	m	l	p	l	r
13	y	s	e	d	r	t	g	f	s	g	z	u	i	o	o
14	b	m	k	l	k	l	o	p	m	n	b	v	g	f	o
15	r	u	e	f	u	l	y	a	s	x	a	d	r	e	k

1. The stadium was littered with the ______________________ of yesterday's rock concert.

2. He paced the hallway looking ______________________ and impatient.

3. In his ______________________, he denied that the company had ignored safety procedures.

4. Don't ______________________ – everything will be alright!

5. Paul still has a ______________________ sense of pride.

6. Joyce regarded his US citizenship as a moral and political ______________________.

7. Kids should learn to sneeze and cough into the ______________________ of their elbows.

8. She gave him a ______________________ smile.

9. His lecture on botany was rather ______________________.

10. The biggest ______________________ in history changed his faith from Islam to Christianity.

While-reading assignments part III, chapter 2

Read part III, chapter 2, on pages 234 – 243.
Answer the following questions.

1. What made América change her mind about perceiving her situation?

2. When did they become aware of the fire?

3. What happened with América as they were lying halfway up the western rim of the canyon?

4. Why was Cándido panicking in that situation?

5. What did Cándido find in one of the gardens of the community and why was he so happy about that?

6. What is the symbolic importance of the appearance of the cat?

Deeper meaning behind quotations – While-reading assignments part III, chapter 3

Read part III, chapter 3, on pages 244 – 253.
In the given grid, there are a number of quotations taken from chapter 3. Write down the deeper meaning behind them.

Statement	Deeper meaning
1. "Turkey?" Kyra lifted her face to fix him with an acid look. "What about the oven, the kitchen, the roof? What about all our furniture, our clothes? Where are we going to live?" (p. 244, ll. 23 ff.)	
2. Jack: "Come on, we can't let these jokers get through," (p. 246, l. 19)	
3. Policeman: "I can handle this." (p. 246, ll. 42 f.)	
4. He stood there a long moment, the gears turning inside him, and when Jack offered the bottle again, he took it. (p. 248, ll. 39 ff.)	
5. Kit: "I found this in my purse. I can't imagine how it got there." (p. 252, ll. 30 f.)	

While-reading assignments part III, chapter 4

While reading part 3, chapter 4, on pages 254 – 263, tick off the correct version of the following statements.

1. Cándido was afraid the fire would be coming closer to the place where he and América were staying because
   - ☐ a) all the people had been evacuated and left their beautiful rich houses behind.
   - ☐ b) he could hear it roar.
   - ☐ c) fires in the area usually went this way.

2. When Cándido was cleaning the baby with a rag he realized that
   - ☐ a) he had a beautiful baby.
   - ☐ b) the baby was a girl, not the son he had hoped for.
   - ☐ c) América had suffered a lot while giving birth.

3. Cándido went into a garden directly behind the wall because
   - ☐ a) he heard a dog barking and wanted to check if anybody was there.
   - ☐ b) América was complaining about having nothing to eat.
   - ☐ c) he desperately had to get food and construction material for a shed.

4. When Cándido wanted América to move away from the dangerous place where they were she
   - ☐ a) was happy to leave the dump.
   - ☐ b) unwillingly followed him.
   - ☐ c) refused and accused him of having betrayed her.

5. When Cándido was dragging the sheet of green-tinted plastic across the lawn, he
   - ☐ a) fell and hurt his leg.
   - ☐ b) was confronted with a vicious dog.
   - ☐ c) saw a woman's face in a window.

6. Looking at América after he had woken up Cándido realized that
   - ☐ a) she would suffer from diarrhea because of all the fruit.
   - ☐ b) she would not be able to nurse her baby any longer.
   - ☐ c) he did not have the slightest chance to get some meat.

While-reading assignments part III, chapter 5

Read part III, chapter 5, on pages 264 – 273 and put the following sentences into the correct order to have a summary of the chapter.

1. They decided to go for a walk before dinner to look for their cat.
2. While they were in the car, the topic of Dominick Flood came up which made Jack Jardine uncomfortable.
3. Delaney developed the film in Jack's darkroom and to his great surprise found that the person tripping the wire had been Cándido.
4. After the fire Kyra drove to the Da Ros place to assess the damage.
5. Jack showed Kyra and Delaney hieroglyphs in graffiti written on both sides of the entrance gate.
6. After watching several nights he was not successful, then skipped a night to find out the following day that both cameras had been tripped.
7. Delaney decided to start nightly vigils with binoculars and two trip-wire cameras to get hold of the sprayers.
8. She was extremely upset and distressed because she held illegal Mexicans responsible for the fire.
9. Having dropped Kit at the airport Delaney met Kyra in their house who was in an agitated state about the loss of the Da Ros place.
10. On their walk they met Jack Jardine in his car who invited them for a lift to show them something.

While-reading assignments part III, chapter 6

1. **While reading pp. 274 – 277 find the following expressions and explain them within the context of the novel.**

   a) under cover of night b) what stinking luck he had c) beyond superstition

   d) the agent of all this destruction e) miracle

   f) like a rabbit in a burrow g) the village priest

2. **While reading pp. 278 ff. find out what América discovers about her baby and what she wants to do about it.**

3. **While reading pp. 276 – 280 finish the following sentences with information from the text.**

   a) América wants to leave the shack and the US again because ______________________________

   ____

   b) Cándido desperately wants to find work, therefore he ______________________________

   ____

   c) When Cándido is waiting at the post office, he encounters several drawbacks:

   ____

   ____

4. **While reading p. 282 write down who Cándido recognizes and explain why he is in such a state of shock.**

   ____

   ____

   ____

Deeper meaning behind quotations – While-reading assignments part III, chapter 7

Read part III, chapter 7, on pages 283 – 296.
In the given grid, there are a number of quotations taken from chapter 7. Write down the deeper meaning behind them.

Statement	Deeper meaning
1. "You!" Delaney shouted. "You stay right there!" (p. 283, l. 1)	
2. "Your vehicle was obstructing the road," the cop said finally, and that was all. (p. 284, ll. 39 f.)	
3. ... when Jack swung round in his seat and said: "Knowing you, I'll bet you're completely naked." (p. 291, ll. 23 f.)	
4. He was breathing hard. He inserted the bullets in the slots so ingeniously designed to receive them, each one sliding in with a precise and lethal click, and he knew he would never use the thing, never fire it, never – (p. 292, l. 29 – l. 32)	
5. It was Jack Jr. and an accomplice Delaney didn't recognize, and there they were, replicated six times on a sheet of contact paper, brought to life, caught in the act. (p. 294, l. 41 – l. 44)	

While-reading assignments part III, chapter 8

Listen to part III, chapter 8, on pages 297, l. 1 – p. 299, l. 30.
a) Tick off the correct version of the following statements.

1. Cándido came back to the shed in a distressed state because
   - ☐ a) he hadn't found any work at all.
   - ☐ b) he had seen Delaney threatening him with a gun.
   - ☐ c) he had seen Delaney who had tried to stop him.

2. América tried to find the right moment to tell Cándido about
   - ☐ a) her fear that the baby might be blind.
   - ☐ b) her worries about their future.
   - ☐ c) her apprehension she might not be able to feed her baby any longer.

3. When something fell against the side of the shack and the flap was wrenched from the doorway
   - ☐ a) a familiar person with a gun looked inside.
   - ☐ b) they saw a coyote standing there.
   - ☐ c) an enormous mudslide hit them.

b) Right, wrong or not in the text.

1. Cándido called Delaney a *gabacho* who would be put in a straitjacket in his village.
2. América smelled no meat in the *cocido*, but potatoes and chiles.
3. When Cándido told América about his encounter with Delaney he remembered that he was wearing a red shirt.
4. América told Cándido the reason why she thought the baby was blind.
5. Cándido treated the baby with a lot of tenderness and care.
6. Delaney's sudden appearance in the door of the hut was a complete shock to both Cándido and América.

Component 4:

Delaney – Racist in a liberal skin

Vor Beginn der Arbeit an diesem *Component* sollte Part III gelesen und inhaltlich erarbeitet worden sein. Die inhaltliche Erarbeitung erfolgt durch *while-reading*-Aufgaben, die auf den letzten Seiten von *Component 3* abgedruckt sind. Die Lösungen zu den *while-reading*-Aufgaben (***Copies 23–30***) folgen an dieser Stelle.

Solutions while-reading assignments part III

While-reading assignments part III, chapter 1

	A	B	C	D	E	F	G	H	I	J	K	L	M	N	O
1	d														
2		e									y	g	d	e	
3			t				o								
4			e	r		d	b							v	
5			s		i	e	s		c	o	n	v	e	r	t
6			t			t	c					s			
7			i			t	u				t				i
8			m			e	r	s		i				n	
9			o			r	e		g				c		
10			n			f		i				u			
11			y				a				b			c	
12						l				u				r	
13									s					o	
14														o	
15	r	u	e	f	u	l								k	

1. The stadium was littered with the ***detritus*** of yesterday's rock concert.
2. He paced the hallway looking ***edgy*** and impatient.
3. In his ***testimony***, he denied that the company had ignored safety procedures.
4. Don't ***fret*** – everything will be alright!
5. Paul still has a ***vestigial*** sense of pride.
6. Joyce regarded his US citizenship as a moral and political ***incubus***.
7. Kids should learn to sneeze and cough into the ***crooks*** of their elbows.
8. She gave him a ***rueful*** smile.
9. His lecture on botany was rather ***obscure***.
10. The biggest ***convert*** in history changed his faith from Islam to Christianity.

While-reading assignments part III, chapter 2

1. She heard a bird calling for its mate and the poignant song made her think of the coming baby and aware that Cándido loved her.
2. América became aware of it after she had driven a stake of oak through the frozen carcass and saw Cándido's shocked face who had apparently seen it before.
3. Her water broke and the birth was starting.
4. He was in panic because he was terrified to help América with the delivery of the baby because he did not have any experience at all.
5. He found a shed with a kerosene lantern to give them light and a faucet with water for him and América.
6. América in her agony regards the cat as a "saint", a "midwife" that gives her some strength in her desperate circumstances.

While-reading assignments part III, chapter 3

Statement	Deeper meaning
1. "Turkey?" Kyra lifted her face to fix him with an acid look. "What about the oven, the kitchen, the roof? "What about all our furniture, our clothes? Where are we going to live?" (p. 244, ll. 23 ff.)	How can you be so stupid and think of a minor thing like a turkey when everything we have is at stake and we might have to face the loss of all our possessions? What a silly joke!
2. Jack: "Come on, we can't let these jokers get through," (p. 246, l. 19)	They are Hispanics and they certainly have something to do with the fire. So we must stop them to find out.
3. Policeman: "I can handle this." (p. 246, ll. 42 f.)	Please don't interfere with my business, this is not your job! Those Anglo Americans are easily ready to put the blame on Mexicans.
4. He stood there a long moment, the gears turning inside him, and when Jack offered the bottle again, he took it. (p. 248, ll. 39 ff.)	Despite his controlled drinking habits he gives in to drinking because he is severely upset about the Mexicans that he thinks started the fire. He needs some type of comfort.
5. Kit: "I found this in my purse. I can't imagine how it got there." (p. 252, ll. 30 f.)	I can't believe that Dominick did that to me – he was so nice and gentlemanlike talking to me all the time. He used me to be able to leave the area – an outrageous thought!

While-reading assignments part III, chapter 4

1 – a; 2 – b; 3 – c; 4 – b; 5 – c; 6 – a

While-reading assignments part III, chapter 5

4 – 8 – 9 – 1 – 10 – 2 – 5 – 7 – 6 – 3

While-reading assignments part III, chapter 6

1. a) under cover of night (p. 274, l. 8): Cándido only dares to move at night because he is afraid to be seen.
   b) what stinking luck he had (p. 274, l. 27): He takes this additional drawback with sarcastic acceptance.
   c) beyond superstition (p. 274, l. 29): He becomes aware of the hopelessness of/his situation that cannot be attributed to any ethical reasoning nor supernatural influence.

d) the agent of all this destruction (p. 275, l. 8): Cándido knows that it is him who is responsible for setting the fire in the canyon.
e) miracle (p. 276, l. 12): América is fascinated by the existence of her baby.
f) like a rabbit in a burrow (p. 276, l. 19): América feels like a hunted animal having to hide and to live in a shack.
g) the village priest (p. 277, l. 23): She wants to follow the rites she knows from her village and translates them to her new circumstances.

2. América discovers that her daughter is blind because the baby does not react to América's hand passing over her daughter's face and only stares. Desperately, América wants to see a doctor to do something about her baby's eyes.
3. a) she realizes that their efforts have been in vain and that there is nowhere to live for them in the US. They live like rabbits in a hole. Moreover, she has a suspicion that her daughter is blind.
   b) walks up to the post office in the rain to look for somebody to give him work.
   c) He has to stand outside in the rain and the cold, the people entering the post office look at him with unrestrained hate, finally a man in a uniform tells him to leave after he has entered the lobby of the office.
4. Cándido recognizes Delaney's car just ahead of him on the shoulder. He is reminded of the terrible accident he suffered and its consequences. He quickly relives the torments he had to experience during the last months. Now he is confronted with him again exposed to Delaney's hatred and fury and is petrified.

While-reading assignments part III, chapter 7

Statement	Deeper meaning
1. "You!" Delaney shouted. "You stay right there!" (p. 283, l. 1)	This time I will get you, you useless son of a bitch! You have made my life miserable enough, I will track you down and make sure the police will take care of this!
2. "Your vehicle was obstructing the road," the cop said finally, and that was all. (p. 284, ll. 39f.)	Don't go on with your prejudices about Hispanics! There is absolutely no evidence of that and I'm fed up with people complaining about them all the time! The only evidence there is that your vehicle was blocking the road which is an offence.
3. ... when Jack swung round in his seat and said: "Knowing you, I'll bet you're completely naked." (p. 291, ll. 23f.)	You as a liberal humanist with your ethical values are certain to not have any weapon in the house because you believe in discussing and talking about things. But when some villain enters your home, you will look fairly stupid.
4. He was breathing hard. He inserted the bullets in the slots so ingeniously designed to receive them, each one sliding in with a precise and lethal click, and he knew he would never use the thing, never fire it, never – (p. 292, l. 29 – l. 32)	Delaney seems to have the gun partly against his will as he does not seem to be prepared to use it to kill anybody. But he wants to use it as a deterrent. However, the line between the two actions is not too solid so he could actually be tempted to fire.
5. It was Jack Jr. and an accomplice Delaney didn't recognize, and there they were, replicated six times on a sheet of contact paper brought to life, caught in the act. (p. 294, ll. 41 – 44)	This is something that Delaney would not have expected as he was prepared to see Cándido's face. However, this does not keep him from tracking down Cándido now. The ironical note is that it is Jack Jardine's son who is the trespasser.

While-reading assignments part III, chapter 8

1 a): 1c); 2a); 3a)
1 b): 1(r); 2(w); 3 (not in the text); 4 (r); 5 (w); 6 (r)

4.1 The wound refusing to heal

Der vierte und letzte *Component* geht auf den gesamten Roman ein, insbesondere jedoch den II. und III. Teil. Das Hauptaugenmerk liegt auf der Figur des Delaney, dessen allmähliche Wandlung vom liberalen Humanisten zum aggressiven Rassisten, hervorgerufen durch die Veränderungen in seiner Umgebung, herausgearbeitet wird. Voraussetzung für die Behandlung dieses *Component* ist, dass der gesamte Roman gelesen wurde, die Kapitel I. 1, I. 3. I. 7, II. 1, II. 3, II. 5, II. 6, III. 3, III. 5, III. 7 und III. 8 intensiv, die restlichen extensiv.
Als Einstieg in den *Component* bietet es sich an, auf der Grundlage der *„1994 California Voter Information: Proposition 187, Text of Proposed Law“* den Schülerinnen und Schülern ***Copy 31*** vorzulegen. Auf diesem Arbeitsblatt sind die wichtigsten Aussagen von *Proposition 187* zusammengestellt und darüber hinaus Argumente dafür und dagegen aufgelistet. Diese können durch Schülerbeiträge noch ergänzt werden. Das Arbeitsblatt kann als Grundlage für eine Diskussion über die Einwandererpolitik in den USA dienen. Im November 1994 stimmten die Kalifornier mit einer Mehrheit von 59 % für *Proposition 187*. Nachdem sie dem Bund zur Abstimmung vorgelegt worden war, wurde sie jedoch von Washington zurückgewiesen.

Read *Copy 31* and find arguments in favour of and against Proposition 187 in order to prepare a discussion. This can be done in an Internet research. Then discuss the given immigration policy in the United States at that time, considering the found arguments.

Das Auffinden von *Pros* und *Cons* kann in Partnerarbeit oder Einzelarbeit unter Zuhilfenahme des Internets erfolgen, die dann anschließend auf Folie oder am Beamer gesammelt werden, was durch eine Schülerin oder einen Schüler geschehen kann. An dieser Stelle wird ein Lösungsvorschlag zu den erarbeiteten Argumenten abgedruckt.

Lösungsvorschlag zu den gefundenen Argumenten *in favour of and against Proposition 187:*

Arguments in favour of Proposition 187

1. California can strike a blow for the taxpayer that will be heard across America; in Arizona, in Texas, in Florida in the same way Proposition 13 was heard across the land.
2. It has been estimated that illegal aliens are costing taxpayers an excess of 5 billion dollars a year.
3. Illegal aliens receive taxpayer – subsidized education including college.
4. Classrooms are overcrowded with illegal children.
5. Illegal aliens are able to buy and sell forged documents without penalty.
6. The State Legislature voted on July 5th to remove dental care as a medical option and force the increase of the cost of prescription drugs for senior citizens. On the other hand, they voted to continue free pre-natal care for illegal aliens.

Arguments against Proposition 187

1. Proposition 187 does not do a thing to beef up the enforcement at the border. It does not even crack down on employers who hire illegal immigrants.
2. Proposition 187 could end up costing taxpayers $ 10 billion.

3. Because Proposition 187 is poorly drafted, it directly conflicts with several important federal laws. As a result, California could lose billions in federal funding. Schools could lose more than $ 3 billion and Medi-Cal for senior and other legal residents could lose $ 7 billion.
4. It requires public school officials to thoroughly verify the citizenship of every child and every parent – more than 10 million people.
5. Proposition 187 would kick 400,000 kids out of school and onto the streets.
6. It threatens the health of all Californians because it would forbid doctors and nurses from giving immunizations or basic medical care to anyone suspected of being an illegal immigrant.
7. Every day, hundreds of thousands of undocumented workers handle the Californians' food supply in the fields and restaurants. Denying them basic health care would only spread communicable diseases throughout the communities and place every Californian citizen at risk.

Es scheint unerlässlich, die weitere Entwicklung in Kalifornien und Arizona bezüglich der Haltung gegenüber illegalen Einwanderern zu betrachten, da inzwischen 20 Jahre vergangen sind und die Einwanderungswellen nicht geringer geworden sind. Dazu wird der auf *Copy 32* abgedruckte Artikel vom 25.6.2013 aus *SFPPR News and Analysis* von Andrew Thomas anhand der im Folgenden angegebenen Aufgabenstellungen erarbeitet. Das methodische Vorgehen erfolgt durch den Ansatz des Experten-Puzzles, d.h., die Schülerinnen und Schüler werden in Dreiergruppen eingeteilt, wobei wiederum jeweils drei dieser Gruppen eine der drei gegebenen Aufgabenstellungen A, B oder C bearbeiten. Anschließend setzen sich die Dreiergruppen auf diese Art neu zusammen, dass in jeder der neu gebildeten Gruppen ein Mitglied aus A, B oder C sitzt. Die Schülerinnen und Schüler informieren sich dann gegenseitig über ihre Ergebnisse, die anschließend noch auf Folie oder Beamer festgehalten werden, um eine generelle Sicherung zu erhalten.

Form groups of three. The given assignments A, B, and C are divided among these groups. So each group works on their assignment. Then different groups of three get together in such a way that in each new group there is one member of A, B, and C. In these new groups the members present their results to each other. Finally, the results are presented on a transparency or on the projector by one member of each assignment group.

Assignments *Copy 32*:

Group A

Answer the following questions:
1. Why have the Mexican border states lost confidence in the ability and willingness of the Federal Government to secure the border? How have they tried to fix the issue themselves? Point out examples.
2. State some of the statements and demands as formulated in *Proposition 187* and describe its impact on Arizona.
3. Point out the reactions on various sides and of various people in the course of the debate about *Proposition 187* and after its passing.

Group B

Answer the following questions:
1. Describe the direct ramifications of the failed proposition for the state of Arizona and point out the state's measures to deal with the situation.

2. What was the reaction of lots of political leaders towards *Proposition 200* in 2004 and what was its final outcome? Point out differences and similarities between the public reception and the federal ruling of *Proposition 187* and *Proposition 200*.
3. State the latest initiatives as to illegal immigration in Arizona and describe their outcome.

Group C

Make a timeline showing the events and ramifications after the first attempt at introducing *Proposition 187* in California in 1994.

Solutions:

Group A

1. They are tired of the current debate of federal immigration reform showing no results. Therefore, they have tried to fix the problem through voter initiatives and referenda, but these efforts have not shown to be a success. In Arizona, there has been a voter-approved requirement of proof of citizenship in order to vote in state elections which was struck down by the U.S. Supreme Court and the federal court in Phoenix. A federal judge in Phoenix found the office of a County Sheriff engaged in racial profiling which does not permit him to go on any further with the federal immigration control business.

2. It noted the "personal injury and damage" and "economic hardship" caused by the "criminal conduct of illegal aliens in this state" pointing out measures and raw material for Arizona's reform efforts some years later. The proposition required police officers to investigate a detainee's immigration status and notify the detainee and federal immigration agents of alien status if determined. The measure forced local government policies that had so far blocked enforcement of this requirement. Moreover, it denied public assistance to all persons not verified by state or local government agencies.

3. There was a wide range of reactions and a lot of controversial reception:
   - the then Governor Pete Wilson based his campaign largely on his support of *Prop 187* and won the election
   - the then President Bill Clinton strongly opposed the referendum
   - in large public protests there were mass boycotts of high schools and a march of more than 70,000 people in downtown Los Angeles
   - governments outside California threatened to boycott the state
   - the then Mexican President denounced the law
   - the ACLU (American Civil Liberties Union) and other groups filed lawsuits after the voters passed *Prop 187*
   - the following Californian Governor Gray Davis dropped the appeal and the reform died after having been ruled as unconstitutional

Group B

1. Operation *Hold the Line* was implemented in El Paso, Texas and *Operation Gatekeeper* was implemented that garrisoned the San Diego Sector of the Border Patrol with fundamentally increased enforcement resources and a sturdy fence. These two led to an increased push of illegal immigrants into Arizona having no defended border with Mexico. So it became the principal corridor of

human smuggling. In 2004 the *Protect Arizona* Initiative, later designated by the state of *Proposition 200* came up containing harsh measures against illegal immigrants. They required individuals to produce proof of citizenship before they could register to vote or receive public benefits and made it a violation against the law for public officials to fail to report persons who sought such benefits but could not produce the required documentation.

2. Almost none of them dared support *Protect Arizona Now* and there was an overwhelming opposition to it. Republican and Democratic leaders marched together in solidarity to oppose the measure. As well there were lots of attack TV ads which further contributed to the denial of the measure. While *Prop 187* had enjoyed a lot of support of even Governor Wilson, anti-illegal-immigration activists in Arizona were not able to raise much money or support.
   Yet, 56 % of Arizonans approved *Prop 200*, among them 47 % of Hispanic voters. But then, in the same way as with *Prop 187* in October 2006, the Federal Court stopped the initiative. In 2013, the voter identification requirements were stopped by the Supreme Court.
3. The claim of Senate Bill 1070 making it a crime to enter Arizona illegally from a foreign country was ruled out at the request of the Obama administration and U.S. Justice Department in 2012. A law prohibiting illegal immigrants from congregating and soliciting work outside home-improvement stores was refuted as well.

Group C

See *Copy 33*: Timeline showing the events and ramifications after the first attempt at introducing Proposition 137 in California in 1994 (solution Group C)

Im Anschluss an die Diskussion kann der Inhalt des ersten Kapitels von *Part I* noch einmal kurz von den Schülerinnen und Schülern zusammengefasst werden. Diese Aufgabe hat wiederholenden Charakter, da dieses Kapitel bereits zusammengefasst und inhaltlich erarbeitet wurde. Um einen Kontrast zur Auseinandersetzung mit der Einwanderungsproblematik auf einer rechtlichen und verallgemeinernden Ebene zu bilden, wird nun das Augenmerk auf die konkrete Gestalt des Delaney gerichtet. Man fährt mit der folgenden Fragestellung fort:

What conflict is there between Delaney's ideals and his behaviour after the accident? (chapter I. 1)

Dalaney's ideals

- liberal-humanist ideals (p. 10)
- feeling of pity for the desperate situation of the Mexican (pp. 15 f.)
- environmentally-friendly person

Dalaney's behaviour

- does not call an ambulance, but offers money to the Mexican (p. 15)
- feeling of outrage against the Hispanics polluting the environment
- lies to the car dealer about the cause of the accident

Write a personal comment about the demands as stated in Proposition 187 on the basis of the discussion held in class.

Nachdem die Hausaufgabe kurz vorgetragen wurde, wird der Inhalt von Kapitel I. 7, welches unter einem anderen Aspekt bereits erarbeitet wurde, kurz von einer Schülerin oder einem Schüler wiedergegeben. Dann werden die Schüler aufgefordert, im *Think-Pair-Share*-Verfahren den Konflikt zwischen Delaneys liberalem Humanismus und seinen konkreten Gefühlen Mexikanern gegenüber, wenn er tatsächlich mit ihnen konfrontiert ist, herauszuarbeiten. An konkreten Beispielen und Situationen sollen Delaneys Gedanken und sein Verhalten bei der Begegnung mit „illegalen“ Mexikanern aufgezeigt werden, z. B. seine Überlegungen nach dem Diebstahl seines Wagens oder seine auffallende Wut beim Anblick des Mülls um das Mexikanercamp herum. Beim *Think-Pair-Share*-Verfahren tauschen sich die Schülerinnen und Schüler zunächst in Partnerarbeit über die Aufgabenstellung aus und einigen sich auf gemeinsame Ergebnisse. Diese werden dann mit einem anderen Schülerpaar verglichen und schließlich zu einem Konsens innerhalb der beiden Gruppen zusammengeführt. Eine Schülerin oder ein Schüler stellt anschließend an der Tafel die gewonnenen Ergebnisse dar, die ihr/ihm von den einzelnen Vierergruppen mitgeteilt werden, um eine Sicherung zu gewährleisten.

Show the conflict between Delaney's ideal of liberal humanism and his feelings and thoughts when confronted with Mexicans (chapter I. 7). Use the *Think-Pair-Share*-method.

Es kann sich folgendes Tafelbild ergeben:

Delaney's ideal of liberal humanism

- tolerant position towards immigrants in the discussion with J. Jardine (pp. 91 ff.)

versus

Delaney's feelings when encountering Mexicans

- Delaney feels anger and shame when meeting the Mexican again, but offers no help (pp. 95 f.)
- Delaney is led into thinking that Cándido threw himself deliberately in front of his car (p. 99)
- desire to destroy the Mexicans' camp because of litter (pp. 101 f.)
- encountering the two Mexicans Delaney wants them to be taken back to Mexico (littering the environment) (p. 105)
- Delaney imagines Cándido behind the driving wheel of his car after the theft (p. 108)

Das Unterrichtsgespräch wendet sich der Unterhaltung zwischen Delaney und J. Jardine Jr. in Kapitel I. 3 zu. Als Einstieg dazu kann man den Abschnitt von Seite 46, Zeile 24 bis Seite 47, Ende vorlesen lassen. Daraufhin werden J. Jardine Jr.'s zentrale Äußerungen und Haltungen Mexikanern gegenüber herausgestellt. Des Weiteren sollte die Aufmerksamkeit der Schüler und Schülerinnen darauf gelenkt werden, dass die von J. Jardine Jr. verbreitete Stimmung als *foreshadowing* der im Folgenden geschilderten Plünderung des Camps angesehen werden kann. Hier kann auf unterstützenden Tafelanschrieb verzichtet werden. Als Hausaufgabe bietet sich an, dass sich die Lerngruppe mit der Widersprüchlichkeit Delaneys auf der Grundlage der im Unterricht erarbeiteten Ergebnisse noch einmal auseinandersetzt.

Comment on the discrepancy between Delaney's deals and his actual behaviour towards Mexicans.

Des Weiteren ist eine *summary* von Kapitel II, 1 zu erstellen.
Zum ersten Teil der Hausaufgabe könnte sich z. B. folgende Ausarbeitung ergeben:

Delaney views Mexicans as types, not as individual human beings. The more contact he has with them, or the more he crosses their path in some way, the more dislike and aggression towards them wells up inside him. Although he does not insult or injure them deliberately, he feels a strong desire to have them removed from the country. His main concern is that the illegal immigrants produce a lot of litter that ruins the landscape.
Delaney is not aware of the discrepancy between his liberal ideals as voiced in his discussion with J. Jardine and his true emotions in actual encounters with Mexican people. An example of this can be seen in the fact that he tries to repress his feelings of guilt towards Cándido by telling himself that Cándido deliberately threw himself in front of his car.

Nach dem Vortragen des 1. Teils der Hausaufgabe (*comment*) werden die Schüler aufgefordert, sich zum Ausdruck *„a wound that refused to heal"* (p. 95, ll. 30 f.) zu äußern. In diesem Unterrichtsgespräch wird der herausragende Aspekt des ersten Teils dieses *Component* noch einmal abschließend herauskristallisiert.

What does "a wound that refused to heal" mean? (chapter I. 7, (p. 95, ll. 30 f.)

Die Ergebnisse lassen sich kurz an der Tafel festhalten:

"A wound that refused to heal"

- since the accident Delaney has seemed to become more aware of the presence of Latin Americans in his "neighbourhood"
- despite the liberal-humanist label he cannot repress feelings of disgust

➡ this conflict opens up a wound inside him

4.2 The long way to racism

Als Einstieg in den zweiten Teil des *Components* wir der zweite Teil der Hausaufgabe, die *summary* von Kapitel II, 1, vorgelesen. Daraufhin richtet sich das Augenmerk auf die Person von Delaney und seinem widersprüchlichen Verhalten und Denken gegenüber Mexikanern. Die Schülerinnen und Schüler werden aufgefordert, sich in einer *creative writing*-Aufgabe in die Person des Delaney, wie er in seiner Entwicklung bis zu Kapitel II, 3 gezeigt wurde, hineinzuversetzen.
Folgende Fragestellung ist denkbar:

Put yourself in the position of Delaney as he has been shown up to chapter II, 3 and describe the inner conflict between your humanist ideals and your actual feelings when encountering Mexicans.

Bei der Bearbeitung dieser Aufgabe sollten folgende Gedanken Delaneys, wie sie in Kapitel II, 3 zum Ausdruck gebracht werden, Erwähnung finden:

> Delaney
> - feels outnumbered by the Mexicans ("Mexicans", Delaney said, and there was no hesitation anymore [...], "there were Mexicans everywhere" (p. 161)
> - still ponders on whether these people have the constitutional right to gather on a street corner (p. 161)
> - wonders if you can assume people are illegal just because they are Mexicans (p. 161)

In der folgenden Stunde liegt der Schwerpunkt auf der Diskussion über Delaneys sich wandelnde Haltung zur Errichtung einer Mauer um das Wohngebiet bzw. zur wachsenden Zahl illegaler Immigranten, wie sie in *chapter II, 6* gezeigt wird. Da drei Begegnungen von zentraler Bedeutung für die Fragestellung sind, bietet es sich an, in arbeitsteiliger Gruppenarbeit Delaneys Streitgespräch mit Kyra, seine Begegnung mit Todd Sweet und seine Begegnung mit dem Mexikaner hinsichtlich seiner Haltung Mexikanern gegenüber zu beleuchten.

> Trace the development of Delaney's position on the building of a wall and the presence of illegal immigrants. (chapter II, 6)

Da die Bearbeitung dieser Aufgabe zu recht ausführlichen Ergebnissen führt, wird auf einen Tafelanschrieb verzichtet. Die Ergebnisse der einzelnen Gruppen werden mündlich vorgetragen, wobei wiederum jede Gruppe aufgefordert ist, die Ergebnisse der jeweils anderen Gruppen zu notieren.

> a) argument between Kyra and Delaney
>   Delaney
>   - resents being blocked out of nature (p. 190)
>   - disagrees with exclusion and division (p. 190)
>   - fears that being walled in will lead to bigotry (p. 194)
>
> b) encounter with Todd Sweet
>   - Delaney agrees that the wall is offensive (p. 195)
>   - when asked for support Delaney suddenly
>   – remembers all the unpleasant incidents involving Mexicans
>   – feels his liberal attitude crumble
>   – dreads fights with Kyra and Jack (p. 196)
>   - answers in an evasive way
>
> c) encounter with the Mexican in his street
>   Delaney
>   - assumes that he is a trespasser (p. 197)
>   - approaches him in an aggressive manner
>   - is shocked about his own behaviour afterwards (p. 198)

Der zweite Teil der Stunde ist der Umsetzung der gefundenen Ergebnisse auf der stilistischen Ebene gewidmet. Dazu kann zur Wiederholung der Fachbegriffe noch einmal kurz ***Copy 21*** eingesetzt werden. Man kann damit fortfahren, den Abschnitt von S. 196, Z. 41 bis S. 198, Z. 5 vorlesen zu lassen. Im Unterrichtsgespräch werden die Stilmittel unter folgender Aufgabenstellung herausgearbeitet:

Identify the stylistic devices that Boyle uses to show Delaney's overreaction to the Mexican in his street. (chapter II, 6)

climax

- "the man looked startled, looked guilty – caught in the act" (p. 196, l. 41)
- "this was the hiker, the illegal camper, [...] Delaney's life" (p. 197, ll. 1 ff.)
- "Delaney was nothing a minor annoyance, [...] round his face" (p. 197, ll. 26 f.)
- "the man was a thief, a liar, [...] a polluter, a Mexican" (p. 197, ll. 36 ff.)

➡ Mexican as the highest gradation

parataxis

- "Delaney was hot. He was uncomfortable. He was aggravated." (p. 197, l. 13)

Im Anschluss kann noch auf Todd Sweet als *telling name* eingegangen werden. *Sweet* kann im Zusammenhang des Romans so gedeutet werden, dass dieser Mann der wachsenden Zahl von Mexikanern freundlich und nicht aggressiv gegenübersteht. Er scheint der Einzige, der die Errichtung einer Mauer um das Wohngebiet ernsthaft verhindern will.

Als Hausaufgabe zur nächsten Stunde eignet sich die Zusammenfassung von Kapitel III, 3.

Um den Schülern ein möglichst umfassendes Bild der Situation in Kapitel III, 3 zu vermitteln, wird das Szenario am Anfang der Stunde um einige geographische Details erweitert, indem *Copy 34* bearbeitet wird.

Im ersten Teil sollten folgende Straßen und Gegenden herausgestellt werden: *Topanga State Park, Topanga Canyon, Topanga Canyon Boulevard, Ventura Boulevard, Sherman Way* und *Canoga Park*.
In der zweiten Aufgabe sollte auf die geographische Nähe zwischen der Wohnstätte der Mexikaner im *Topanga Canyon* und der *gated community* der Weißen hingewiesen werden. Obwohl beide so nahe beieinander liegen, gestalten sich die jeweiligen Wohnverhältnisse völlig konträr zueinander: luxuriöses, abgeschottetes Inseldasein auf der einen und kümmerliches Dahinvegetieren auf der anderen Seite. Beide Gebiete liegen nicht weit von Malibu entfernt, was zum gegenwärtigen Zeitpunkt als eines der attraktivsten und teuersten Wohngebiete Kaliforniens gilt. Zudem ist durch die topographische Darstellung von *Sherman Way* und *Canoga Park* zu ermessen, wie lang und beschwerlich ein Fußweg vom Canyon dorthin für Cándido und América gewesen sein muss.
In der Schöningh-Textausgabe des Romans *The Tortilla Curtain* (Best.-Nr. 041282-7) finden sich im Anhang statistische Informationen zu den einzelnen Wohngebieten (Bevölkerungsdichte, ethnische Zusammensetzung der Bewohner, Einkommen, Bildung), die zur Bearbeitung von Aufgabe 2 herangezogen werden könnten.

In der folgenden Stunde wird anhand einer Textstelle Delaneys deutliche Wandlung zum Rassisten unter Betrachtung einiger möglicher Ursachen erarbeitet. Als Alternative zu diesem Vorgehen kann man diesen Themenkomplex aus dem Unterricht herausnehmen und ihn im Rahmen einer Klausur behandeln lassen (s. Klausuren).

Read excerpt p. 245, l. 34 – p. 248, l. 41. Together with a partner find passages in this excerpt in which Delaney's racist behaviour comes to surface. Give reasons for this change (chapter III. 3). Then use your findings to follow the procedure of the "hot seat" in which one student enacts the role of Delaney on the "hot seat" and the others ask him questions about his changed attitude towards the presence of the Hispanics and the reasons leading to this.

Bei dem methodischen Vorgehen des *hot seat* versetzt sich eine Schülerin bzw. ein Schüler in die Rolle des Delaney, während die anderen diese Person zu ihrer Haltung bzw. den dazu vorliegenden Motiven befragen. Dieses Vorgehen kann mit unterschiedlichen Personen auf dem *hot seat* durchgeführt werden, wobei man anschließend auch eine Evaluierung der jeweiligen *hot seat*-Vertreter vornehmen kann, um ihnen dadurch ein Feedback geben zu können.

Delaney's racist behaviour

Delaney

- is full of hatred on seeing the Latinos (pp. 245 f.)
- tells the police a lie (p. 246)
- attacks the Mexican without feeling guilty (p. 248)

Reasons

- accumulation of unfortunate occurrences related to Mexicans
  - car crashing into Cándido
  - theft of car
  - Kyra's fear on encountering the Latinos
  - fight over wall
- consumption of alcohol
- Arroyo Blanco inhabitants turning into a mob
- raging fire
- deep fear of loss of possessions

➡ attempt at finding a scapegoat

Eine geeignete Hausaufgabe zur nächsten Stunde besteht darin, Delaneys Verhaltensänderungen bei der Begegnung mit José und seinem Freund im Canyon, mit dem Zeitungsausträger und schließlich mit José und seinem Freund während des Feuers aufzuzeigen (Kapitel I, 7, II, 6, III, 3).
In der folgenden Stunde wird eine abschließende Betrachtung der Person des Delaney hinsichtlich seiner vollkommenen Wandlung in einen blinden Rassisten aufgezeigt, der von der Vorstellung besessen ist, den illegalen mexikanischen Einwanderer Cándido unter allen Umständen zu stellen. Zunächst wird im Unterrichtsgespräch der Inhalt der Kapitel III, 6, III, 7 und III, 8 skizziert. Alternativ können Zusammenfassungen zu den genannten Kapiteln von einzelnen Schülerinnen und Schülern im Rahmen einer Hausaufgabe angefertigt werden. Im nächsten Schritt werden die Kapitel III, 6, 7, 8 unter folgender Fragestellung beleuchtet:

What are Delaney's ultimate steps and actions that show his complete transformation into a racist stalking Mexicans? (chapter III, 6/7/8)

Stalking the Mexicans

- exposing Cándido with the help of trip-wire cameras (p. 273)
- accosting Cándido on the road leading to the damage to Delaney's car (pp. 283 f.)
- acquisition of gun (p. 292)
- ignoring evidence presented by cameras (pp. 294 f.)
- finally tracking down the Mexicans in the shack (pp. 299 f.)

➡ ultimate catastrophe

Es sollte an dieser Stelle noch auf einige symbolische Aspekte im letzten Kapitel eingegangen werden. Die Szene in der Hütte mit Cándido, América und dem Baby kann im biblischen Sinne als *Nativity Scene* angesehen werden, während die durch die schweren Regengüsse hervorgerufene *mudslide* zu einer Katastrophe führt, die man in einer ähnlichen Interpretation als *doomsday* ansehen kann.

Um die Lerngruppe abschließend zu einer kritischen Stellungnahme zum Roman bzw. zum Formulieren der persönlichen Eindrücke nach der Lektüre anzuregen, kann die Rezension *The Pilgrim of Topanga Creek* aus der *New York Times* vom 3.9.1995 (URL: www.nytimes.com/books/98/02/08/home/boyle-tortilla.html [10.05.16)] vorgelegt werden. Alternativ kann man diese Rezension auch als Teil einer Klausur behandeln.

Comment on this critic's words.

Die Bearbeitung dieser Aufgabe hängt stark vom persönlichen Leseeindruck der einzelnen Schülerin oder des einzelnen Schülers ab und lässt insofern keinen fest abgegrenzten Erwartungshorizont zu.
Man kann sich mit der Meinung des Kritikers einverstanden erklären und an Beispielen belegen, warum man die Protagonisten Delaney und Kyra für farblos gestaltet hält. Es lassen sich Belege dafür finden, dass Boyle sich im Roman an manchen Stellen über diese beiden Figuren regelrecht lustig macht, indem er einzelne Verhaltensweisen oder Charakterzüge überzeichnet, also eine ironische Distanz wahrt. Des Weiteren lassen sich konstruierte ironische Verflechtungen herausstellen, wie z. B. Cándido's Arbeit an einer Mauer, die gebaut wird, um Menschen wie seinesgleichen abzuhalten. Das Ende des Romans kann man als unglaubwürdig und unwahrscheinlich ansehen. Zum einen wird der Roman jäh und unerwartet beendet, zum anderen kann die Frage nach der literarischen Sinnhaftigkeit der Rettung Delaneys durch Cándido gestellt werden.
Auf der anderen Seite kann man eine andere Position als die des Kritikers einnehmen und herausstellen, dass die Figuren América und Cándido glaubwürdig und authentisch gestaltet sind. Es gelingt Boyle, ihre schwierigen Lebensumstände und die daraus resultierenden Versuche, aus einer verzweifelten Situation herauszukommen, plastisch und bewegend zu schildern. Es werden typisch lateinamerikanische Denkweisen an die Oberfläche gebracht, wie z. B. Cándidos innere Abneigung dagegen, dass er als Mann eine Zeit lang nicht für den Lebensunterhalt aufkommen kann. Der Autor beweist als Anglo-Amerikaner ein großes Einfühlungsvermögen in das Denken und Fühlen von Mexikanern.

Proposition 187: Main statements – excerpts

1. The People of California find and declare as follows:
   a) That they have suffered and are suffering economic hardship caused by the presence of illegal aliens in this state.
   b) That they have suffered and are suffering personal injury and damage caused by the criminal conduct of illegal aliens in this state.
   c) That they have a right to the protection of their government from any person or persons entering this country unlawfully.
   d) Therefore, the People of California declare their intention to provide for cooperation between their agencies of state and local government with the federal government, and to establish a system of required notification, by and between such agencies to prevent illegal aliens in the United States from receiving benefits or public services in the state of California.

2. Every law enforcement agency in California shall fully cooperate with the United States Immigration and Naturalization Service regarding any person who is arrested if he or she is suspected of being present in the United States in violation of federal immigration laws.

3. In order to carry out the intention of the People of California that only citizens of the United States and aliens lawfully admitted to the United States may receive the benefits of public social services and to ensure that all persons employed in the providing of those services shall diligently protect public funds from misuse, the provisions of this section are adopted.

4. In order to carry out the intention of the People of California that, excepting emergency medical care as required by federal law, only citizens of the United States and aliens lawfully admitted to the United States may receive the benefits of publicly-funded health care, and to ensure that all persons employed in the providing of those services shall diligently protect public funds from misuse, the provisions of this section are adopted.

5. No public elementary or secondary school shall admit, or permit the attendance of and no public institution of post secondary education shall admit, enroll, or permit the attendance of any person who is not a citizen of the United States, an alien lawfully admitted as a permanent resident in the United States, or a person who is otherwise authorized under federal law to be present in the United States.

(1994 California Voter Information: Proposition 187, Text of Proposed Law)

Proposition 187: Arizona's page from California's illegal immigration playbook

Read the online article by Andrew Thomas: *Propositon 187: Arizona's page from California's illegal immigration playbook:*
URL: http://sfppr.org/2013/06/proposition-187-arizonas-page-from-californias-illegal-immigration-playbook

Here are some annotations to help with the vocabulary:

ramifications	the possible results of an action
referendum	an occasion when all the people in a country can vote in order to show their opinion about a political question
ligitation	the process of taking a case to the court of law so that a judgment can be made
porous	not protected enough to stop people going through
partisan	strongly supporting a person, principle, or political party
to forestall	to prevent something from happening by acting first
ACLU	American Civil Liberties Union
in limbo	in a situation where you do not know what will happen or when something will happen
U.S. Court of Appeals	*Berufungsgericht*
contortion	violent and unnatural twist into a different shape or form
populist	representing or connected with the ideas and opinions of ordinary people
misdemeanor	an immoral action
AFL-CIO	the American Federation of Labour and Congress of Industrial Organizations
onslaught	very powerful attack
coup de grace	an action that ends something that has been gradually getting worse
Ninth Circuit of Appeals	hears appeals of cases decided by executive branch agencies and federal trial courts in nine western states and two Pacific island jurisdictions
home-improvement store	*Baumarkt*

Assignments

Form groups of three. The given assignments A, B, and C are divided among these groups. So each group works on their assignment. Then different groups of three get together in such a way that in each new group there is one member of A, B, and C. In these new groups the members present their results to each other. Finally, the results are presented on a transparency or on the projector by one member of each assignment group.

Group A

Answer the following questions:

1. Why have the Mexican border states lost confidence in the ability and willingness of the Federal Government to secure the border? How have they tried to fix the issue themselves? Point out examples.
2. State some of the statements and demands as formulated in *Proposition 187* and describe its impact on Arizona.
3. Point out the reactions on various sides and of various people in the course of the debate about *Proposition 187* and after its passing.

Group B

Answer the following questions:

1. Describe the direct ramifications of the failed proposition for the state of Arizona and point out the state's measures to deal with the situation.
2. What was the reaction of lots of political leaders towards *Proposition 200* in 2004 and what was its final outcome? Point out differences and similarities between the public reception and the federal ruling of *Proposition 187* and *Proposition 200*.
3. State the latest initiatives as to illegal immigration in Arizona and describe their outcome.

Group C

Make a timeline showing the events and ramifications after the first attempt at introducing *Proposition 187* in California in 1994.

Timeline showing the events and ramifications after the first attempt at introducing Proposition 187 in California in 1994 (solution Group C)

Arizona

Date	2004	November 2004	October 2006	2012	June 2013
Event	Arizonans come up with Protect *Arizona Now or Proposition 200*	Voters approved *Prop 200* with 56 %	Ninth Circuit Court of Appeals stopped Arizona from requiring voter documentation at the polls	The U.S. Supreme Court threw out the provision that made it a crime to enter Arizona illegally from a foreign country, the heart of Senate Bill 1070	The U.S. Supreme Court and U.S. District Court ruled that *Protect Arizona Now's* voter identification requirements and Sheriff Arpaio's attempts to enforce immigration should not be put into effect

California

Date	8 November 1994	1997
Event	Voters approved *Prop 187* with 59 %	*Pro 187* was ruled out as unconstitutional by a federal judge

1. Identify the places mentioned in the book.
2. Comment on the contrast of the respective living areas.

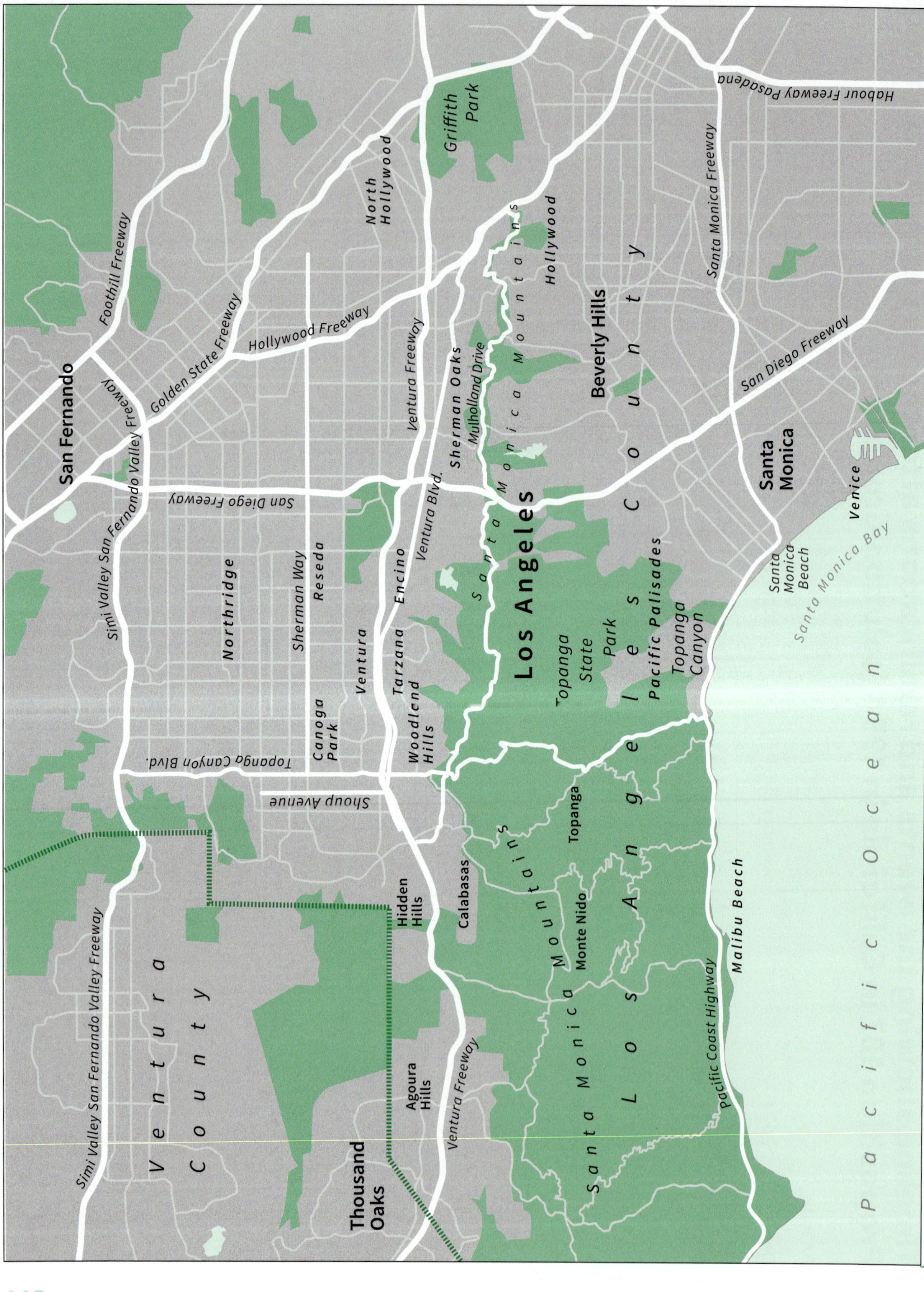

Component 5

Looking back and beyond

Nachdem die eigentliche Arbeit mit dem Roman abgeschlossen ist, bietet es sich an, das im Rahmen der Reihe erworbene Wissen der Schülerinnen und Schüler in den anschließenden Stunden zu festigen und zu erweitern. Dazu werden im Folgenden verschiedene Materialien vorgestellt, die auch als Lerntheke oder Lernzirkel arrangiert werden können.

Auf ***Copy 35*** sind eine Reihe von Begriffen in Kästchen abgedruckt, die einen direkten Bezug zu *The Tortilla Curtain* haben und kopiert, laminiert und ausgeschnitten werden sollten. Dann werden diese Kärtchen mit dem Begriff nach unten auf dem Pult ausgebreitet und ein Schüler kommt nach vorne, wählt ein Kärtchen aus und spricht dann möglichst lange zu dem Begriff und seinem Bezug zum Roman. (*Touch, Turn, Talk*-Methode). Dann nimmt er den nächsten Schüler an die Reihe.

Anhand der Tabelle auf ***Copy 36*** können die Schüler ihre Reaktionen reflektieren und erläutern, die die verschiedenen Figuren des Romans in ihnen auslösen. Dabei füllen sie die Tabelle nach ihren persönlichen Vorstellungen zunächst in Einzelarbeit aus. Sie sollten darauf aufmerksam gemacht werden, dass nicht jede Zeile aufgefüllt werden muss und sie auch die Leerzeile für eigene Ergänzungen nutzen können. Dann tauschen sie ihre Erfahrungen zu zweit oder in Kleingruppen aus, während sie einen kurzen Spaziergang z. B. über den Schulhof machen (*walking while talking*-Methode).
Auf ***Copy 37*** findet sich eine Postkarte aus Kalifornien, die einen direkten Bezug zu im Roman angesprochenen Themen aufweist: *mudslides, fires, riots*. Sie soll den Schülern Gelegenheit bieten, ihre Mündlichkeit zu trainieren, indem sie einen Kurzvortrag von zwei Minuten vorbereiten und halten.

Die nächste Aufgabe (***Copy 38***) besteht aus einer *Listening Comprehension*-Übung mit einem podcast als Grundlage. In diesem geht es um die Haltung der *National Hispanic Medical Association* zur Krankenversicherung für illegale hispanische Einwanderer und ihre Krankenversicherungssituation im allgemeinen. Als Einstieg in die Arbeit mit dem *podcast* wird die *„true/false/not in the text"*-Tabelle verteilt und der *podcast* zweimal vorgespielt, sodass es ausreichend Zeit gibt, die vorgestellten Aussagen einzustufen. Der im *podcast* gesprochene Text ist auch als Transkript abgedruckt. Die Aufnahme kann unter http://www.npr.org/templates/story/story.php?storyId=113107192 im Internet abgerufen werden.

Podcast: NPR Health care

Hispanics in the U.S. are likely to be uninsured

September 23, 2009 (3 min 44 sec)

Transcript

Congress is considering bills that would help provide health insurance to millions of Americans who don't have it. If this happens, one of the big beneficiaries would be Hispanics. One third of all Hispanics in the U.S. are uninsured. Dr. Elena Rios, president of the National Hispanic Medical Association, tells Linda Wertheimer that millions are uninsured because of cultural reasons as well as economic ones.

LINDA WERTHEIMER, host:

The current Congress is considering bills that would help provide health insurance to millions of Americans who don't have it. If this comes about, one of the big beneficiaries would be Hispanics. A third of all Hispanics in the U.S. are uninsured. Dr. Elena Rios is president of the National Hispanic Medical Association. She says there are cultural reasons, as well as economic ones.

Dr. ELENA RIOS (President, National Hispanic Medical Association): Hispanics have health beliefs that are unique, lots of traditional ways of taking care of disease with teas and herbs and other things. And so families don't send their children or young adults to doctors. Another reason is other Hispanics come from other countries where their government provides health insurance.

WERTHEIMER: So they don't ...

Dr. RIOS: They don't ...

WERTHEIMER: ... expect to have to pay for it themselves.

Dr. RIOS: Right. And there's also the trust factors. Hispanics cannot entrust these authority figures, and let alone government, because we have mixed families with undocumented grandparents who don't want to be deported back to where they come from.

WERTHEIMER: What, then, do you think would be the change that would be most important for this population?

Dr. RIOS: I think access to health care services by having affordable health insurance. Of course, there would have to be lots of education and outreach of the importance of purchasing health insurance.

WERTHEIMER: Sort of just get them on the insurance rolls, that would make the difference.

Dr. RIOS: Well, it's not only getting them on the insurance rolls. It's also we need the Hispanics to become the doctors and nurses in the clinics and in the hospitals in the communities that are going to have increased demand.

WERTHEIMER: One of the questions that was raised in some of those fairly obstreperous town meetings that were held over the summer about health care reform was about coverage of illegal immigrants. Now the president says it's not happening. Do you think it should? Is leaving them out going to cause some kind of consequence that we – that we need to take note of?

Dr. RIOS: Well, I think the consequence of leaving them out is that there will be more sickness carried by persons who are in our restaurants, who work in our hotels, who work in our communities that can impact every American citizen.

WERTHEIMER: Does your organization take a position on ensuring illegal immigrants?

Dr. RIOS: No, our organization agrees with President Obama to have this health care reform system be changed for American citizens and those eligible to participate for health reform, and that does not include illegal and undocumented.

WERTHEIMER: What about people who are in this country legally – not citizens, but here legally, working legally. Should they be covered?

Dr. RIOS: Yes, and in order to increase access to as many eligible people as possible in our communities, especially with Hispanic undocumented who have become legal, we feel that they should have access on day one, as everyone else would.

WERTHEIMER: Dr. Rios, this – and I know this has been a huge concern of yours, that there are so many people that don't have access to health care in the Hispanic community in the United States. Do you think that the kinds of health care plans the Congress is looking at will settle that?

DR. RIOS: Well, I think that it's a first step in allowing an affordable health insurance system to be created. You know, 25 percent of the country is about to become Hispanic. We only have 5 percent Hispanic doctors, 2 percent Hispanic nurses. So to have cultural competence training targeted to populations like the Hispanic family and the Hispanic community is a very big success story yet to be seen.

WERTHEIMER: Dr. Rios, thanks very much for talking to us.

Dr. RIOS: Thank you.

WERTHEIMER: Dr. Elena Rios is president of The National Hispanic Medical Association.

Lösungen zu *Copy 38*:

Statements	true	false	not in the text
1. Many Hispanics are uninsured because of cultural and economic reasons.	X		
2. Hispanics coming from countries where health insurance is provided are aware of the fact that they have to pay for it in the US.		X	
3. Health care services for Hispanics should be provided if the health insurance rates are affordable.	X		
4. In areas where there is increased demand for medical services doctors and nurses of Hispanic origin should work in the clinics and hospitals.	X		
5. There are no consequences for any American citizen if illegal immigrants are covered by an insurance or not.		X	
6. The National Hispanic Association is an important advisor of President Obama.			X
7. According to the National Hispanic Association undocumented Hispanics who have become legal should have access to medical services.	X		
8. The US have 7 percent Hispanic doctors and 2 percent Hispanic nurses.		X	

Auf *Copy 39* finden sich Hinweise zum Vorgehen bei der Cartoonanalyse, auf denen zudem sprachliches Material zur Verfügung gestellt wird. Auf *Copy 40* werden drei Cartoons angeboten, die sich mit dem Thema der hispanischen Einwanderung in die USA beschäftigen und diese ironisch beleuchten. Zunächst wird *Copy 39* mit dem Kurs besprochen und anschließend können einige der abgedruckten Cartoons in Partnerarbeit oder der Methode der „Expertengruppen" analysiert werden.

Zum Thema „Illegal immigration" und „Hispanics in the US" gibt es eine Reihe von YouTube Videos, die als Ergänzung und zur breiteren Diskussion zum Thema eingesetzt werden können. Im Folgenden werden einige Internetadressen mit den zugehörigen Titeln genannt:

1. **World: Trapped in Tijuana**
   https://www.youtube.com/watch?v=TgsBlklNxBo
2. **Welcome to Tijuana**
   https://www.youtube.com/watch?v=6FO_NTEudfI
3. **Hispanics in California now outnumber whites – BBC news**
   https://www.youtube.com/watch?y=hcCudotri0E

Die Rede (gekürzt auf *Copy 42*), die Julián Castro, Bürgermeister von San Antonio (mexikanischen Ursprungs), auf der letzten *Democratic National Convention* (2012) gehalten hat, um für die Wiederwahl Barack Obamas zum Präsidenten zu werben, handelt vom American Dream und sollte über das Hörverstehen präsentiert werden. Sie kann unter folgenden Links heruntergeladen oder auch angesehen werden.

mp3 download: www.npr.org/2012/09/04/160574895/transcript-julian-castros-dnc-keynote-address
Video: www.youtube.com/watch?v=GSvEOEB7UW0

Die Hörverstehensaufgaben auf *Copy 41* lassen Teile der Rede außer Acht und so sollten die auf der Transkription (*Copy 42*) ausgewiesenen Kürzungen aus dem Hörtext ausgeschnitten (z. B. mit dem kostenlosen Programm *audacity*) oder die Schüler darauf aufmerksam gemacht werden.

Lösungen zu *Copy 41*:

1. Now listen to the speech for the first time and tick if the statements are true, false or not in the text.

statement	true	false
a) Castro's grandmother had to leave her San Antonio school after the fourth grade because her family moved back to Mexico.		X
b) In America, everybody has the chance to upward movement.	X	
c) Previous generations have acted with far-sightedness to improve their children's lives.	X	
d) Castro's high school classmates in San Antonio did not have the same motivation to succeed in life as his fellow students at Stanford and Harvard university.		X
e) The Democratic Party will not support the outsourcing of jobs.	X	
f) If President Obama is re-elected, America will prosper.	X	

2. While listening to the speech for a second time, finish the following sentences according to the speech in note form.

1. To be able to give her daughter a better life, Castro's grandmother worked hard as a
   a) maid b) cook c) babysitter
2. The hard work of former generations made the following things possible:
   a) decent jobs b) secure retirement
   c) chance for children
3. The American middle class stands for economic growth
4. To have a chance for a good life, it is essential to get a good education.
5. Many immigrants are menaced by deportation.
6. The Democratic Party will not make millionaires even richer by taking the money from the middle class.
7. In the past, America has been able to prevail with the wisdom of its founders and familiy values.

3. Castro's speech is a keynote speech, a speech intended to set the underlying tone and summarize the core message of the Democratic National Convention.

a) Describe the tone of his speech in one word. optimistic
b) Point out the core message of his speech.

With Obama as president, America will be able to solve its problems of unemployment, health care, illegal immigration and improve education for all. America will remain the country of opportunities for everybody.

Der Song *Frijolero* der mexikanischen Gruppe Molotov beschäftigt sich mit den Haltungen mexikanischer Einwanderer zu US Amerikanern und umgekehrt. Es ist ein bilingualer Song, in dem beide Seiten zu Wort kommen und auch stereotype Beschimpfungen (z. T. in anstößigen Worten) aufgegriffen werden. Der Titel ist die mexikanische Übersetzung des Schimpfwortes *beaner* („Bohnenfresser"), mit dem US Amerikaner gelegentlich Mexikaner betiteln. So auch in *The Tortilla Curtain*, wo América und Cándido am Ende von Teil I, Kapitel 4 ihr Camp zerstört und die Botschaft *„Beaners Die"* in blutroten Buchstaben auf die Felsen gesprüht finden. Der aggressive Ton des Songs wird durch folkloristische Elemente der *música norteña*, abgeschwächt. *Frijolero* wurde 2003 für den *Latin Grammy* in der Rubrik „Bester Rock Song" nominiert. Das Video gewann den *Grammy Latino* und den MTV VMALA Preis als bestes Video des Jahres 2003 und kann unter folgender Adresse angesehen werden:
www.dailymotion.com/video/x27m1k_molotov-frijolero_music

Der Song wird zunächst mit Unterstützung von ***Copy 43*** über das Hörverstehen präsentiert. Für die tiefergehenden Aufgaben, die auf Perspektive und Sprachgebrauch fokussieren, ist die Textvorlage erforderlich. Da davon ausgegangen werden kann, dass viele Schüler auch Spanischunterricht erhalten, wird auch eine trilinguale Mediationsaufgabe angeboten. Dabei ist zu beachten, dass die zu mittelnden Textstellen von deutlich unterschiedlicher Länge und Schwierigkeitsgrad sind. Für eine gelungene Übertragung des Inhaltes müsste der Sprachmittler an einigen Stellen kulturelle Zusatzinformationen liefern, die er zum Teil in den *annotations* auf ***Copy 44*** finden kann. Die Präsentation der Bilder (Aufgabe 6) eignet sich für einen *gallery walk* (Museumsgang). Alle Schüler stellen ihre Bilder (mit dem kurzen Text) an geeigneter Stelle aus. Dann sehen sie sich die Werke der anderen an und kommen ins Gespräch.

Lösungsvorschläge zu *Copy 43*

1. The students will probably expect some kind of aggressive rap, hip-hop or rock music. The theme of the song seems to be the violent clash of two persons of different attitudes/opinions/goals.

2. Individual answers. The song is about the tense relations between Mexican immigrants and US Americans (at the border).

3. Correct order: 8 – 3 – 1 – 7 – 5 – 9 – 4 – 6 – 10 – 2

4. The song uses an alternating point of view: a Mexican immigrant is speaking in Spanish to an American border patrol officer who addresses him in English. The same can be said about the refrain which also switches between the two points of view and languages. Then the Mexican also uses the English language (ll. 29 – 36 and ll. 45 – 49) to express his outrage. From the facts that the Spanish part is sung with an American accent and that the Mexican also speaks English you may conclude that the Mexican is an immigrant who has lived for a long time in the US. It is interesting to note that the Mexican speaks an English free of accent and is able to switch easily from one language to the other. He even uses both languages in one sentence (l. 43). This reveals that he knows about the American society and culture while the American seems to be ignorant of Mexico. He only uses the word *gringo* pronounced with an American accent to react to the Mexican *frijolero*.

5 a) Mediation of the English parts into Spanish
- ll. 17 – 22: El americano le exige al mejicano que no le llame "gringo", pero al mismo tiempo le insulta con la palabra "fijolero" y le grita de quedarse a su lado del río. Se está refiriendo al Río Bravo (río Grande en inglés) que forma en gran parte la frontera entre Méjico y los Estados Unidos.
- ll. 29 – 36: El mejicano dice que sería muy rico si hubiera recibido 10 centavos por cada vez que le miraron feo por estar al lado equivocado de la ciudad. Pro

bablemente se refiere a una de las ciudades gemelas que se extienden por los dos lados de la frontera como por ejemplo Ciudad Juarez en Méjico y El Paso en Estados Unidos. Últimamente el mejicano está furioso por eso y tiene ganas de pegar a estos racistas.

5. b) Mediation of the Spanish parts into English

- ll. 1 – 16: The Mexican says that he is sick and tired of being called "beaner". He blames the USA of making profit from the wars they start in other countries, alluding to the US invasion of Iraq in 2003. He states the Mexicans pay their depths with oil, even though they don't know who will really get the money. He mentions the drug production the Americans accuse the Mexicans of, only to accuse the Americans of being the consumers of these drugs.
- ll. 3 – 28: The Mexican addresses the American in an aggressive tone, using slang swear words to stop him insulting him and to menace him for being a racist.
- ll. 27 – 50: In these lines the Mexican asks the American to adopt the perspective of an illegal Mexican immigrant and explains how difficult it is to leave everything behind and start from nothing and how dangerous it is to cross the border because the Americans shoot at him. Then he reminds the American of the fact that Texas had been Mexican territory until 1936, referring to Santa Ana, a Mexican politician who is responsible for the loss.

5. c) Mediation of the Spanish and English parts into German.

Der Song handelt von den angespannten Beziehungen zwischen US Amerikanern und mexikanischen Einwanderern in der Grenzregion. Der Mexikaner fordert den Amerikaner auf, ihn nicht länger zu beschimpfen und wirft Amerika vor, sich durch Krieg mit anderen Ländern zu bereichern. Dabei spielt er auf die Invasion des Irak durch amerikanische Truppen im Jahr 2003 an. Der Mexikaner entkräftet den Vorwurf des Drogenanbaus mit dem Verweis auf die amerikanischen Konsumenten. Im Refrain verlangt der amerikanische Grenzpolizist, nicht mehr beleidigt zu werden, fügt aber gleich selber eine Beleidigung hinzu. Er befiehlt dem Mexikaner, auf seiner Seite des verfluchten Flusses zu bleiben. Er meint den Rio Bravo, der über viele Kilometer die Grenze zwischen den USA und Mexiko bildet. Daraufhin stößt der Mexikaner unflätige Drohungen aus. Der mexikanische Einwanderer beklagt sich über die feindselige Reaktion, die ihm entgegenschlägt, wenn er sich auf der falschen Seite der Stadt aufhält. Wahrscheinlich bezieht er sich hier auf die Zwillingsstädte Ciudad Juarez (Mexiko) und El Paso (Texas, USA), die sich über beide Staaten ausbreiten. Dann bittet er den Amerikaner sich vorzustellen, wie schwer es für den Auswanderer ist, alles zurückzulassen und bei Null wieder anzufangen. Außerdem ist es lebensgefährlich, die Grenze zu überqueren, weil auf die Illegalen geschossen wird. Zum Schluss erinnert er den Amerikaner daran, dass Texas bis 1936 zu Mexiko gehörte, indem er auf den mexikanischen Politiker Santa Ana verweist, durch dessen Fehlverhalten das Gebiet verloren ging.

6. individual answers

Copy 45 bietet einen deutschen Text, der das Schicksal junger Einwanderer, die bereits als Kinder mit ihren Eltern illegal in die USA eingewandert sind, beschreibt. Die Aufgabe der Schülerinnen und Schüler besteht darin, einem Freund aus Kalifornien zu berichten, was man in Deutschland über das Problem weiß.

Lösungsvorschlag zu *Copy 45*

Students should point out that according to the article there are about 12 million illegal Hispanic immigrants living in the US. There are many young people whose parents brought them to the US as children and who are still living there without papers. They can go to school, but they cannot get a driver's license. They drive cars anyway and hope that they will not be stopped by the police. They find jobs that are not well paid and work hard. Since it is dangerous for them to be found out not many people know about the fact that they are illegal. When detected they will be sent back to Mexico or other countries in Middle or South America. President Obama wants to give many of these people a chance to become legal immigrants and prepares a new law that will make it possible for illegal immigrants to come out of their hiding places and get papers. The conditions are easy to fulfil: They must have lived in the US for 5 years or longer, they must not have a record and they must have graduated from high school.

Als letztes bietet *Component 5* zwei *blog entries*, die die Reaktionen zweier Leser auf den Roman widerspiegeln. Die Aufgabe besteht darin, die Meinungen der Leser zu verstehen und im Anschluss daran, selber eine solche Rezension zu verfassen.

Lösungsvorschlag zu *Copy 46*

Task 1

George likes the novel very much and calls it a "gripping story" (l. 1). He calls Boyle's writing "a good read" (ll. 2/3) and likes the way the story is told speaking of its "breath taking style" (l. 14). He says that the topic is still important and that the insight we gain into the lives of illegal immigrants is meaningful because there are many people living in the US who share Cándido's and América's fate.
Susan, on the other hand, does not like the book at all. She criticizes its characters and feels bored by its story which she compares to the film "Groundhog Day" in which the protagonist goes through the same day again and again. She could not identify with or feel compassion for the characters and so she had a hard time reading the book. She even recommends another movie, "The Visitor", because it shows the problem of illegal immigration in a more convincing way.

Task 2

Answers will vary but students should give reason for their praise or criticism.

Touch Turn Talk

accident	Arroyo Blanco	Delaney
liberal humanist	Topanga Canyon	coyote
Pilgrim	Kenny Grissom	Kyra
20$	labor exchange	Candelario Pérez
Tepoztlán	La Migra	Jordan
Wide Open Spaces	Jack Jardine	Jack Cherrystone
Resurrección	Tijuana	border

Mary	"Beaners die"	Venice
Sacheverell	Osbert	married woman
eyes the color of calf's liver	camp	25$
gate	being cheated	buddha
Da Ros place	pasta	Jack Jardine Jr.
the Tortilla Curtain	wetback	*gabacho*
José Navidad	hike	stolen car

Kit Menaker	ankle monitoring device	Dominick Flood
El Teenksgeevee turkey	fire in the canyon	cat as a midwife
two Mexicans walking up from the canyon	the riot	the birth
the daughter	camera	blind baby
at the post office	graffiti on the wall next to the gate	trip wire cameras
“There is no money.”	Jack Jardine Jr.	“I saw a ghost.”
“You stay right there!”	the *gabacho* face	the mudslide

The effect *The Tortilla Curtain* has on the reader

After reading the novel *The Tortilla Curtain*, what do you feel?

I feel ...	For whom?	Why?
sympathy		
respect		
understanding		
indignation		
amusement		
sadness		
anger		
hope		
fear		
incomprehension		
contempt		
...		

Giving a three-minute talk

Describe the postcard in detail.
Comment on its relation to the novel *The Tortilla Curtain*.
Be prepared to give a three-minute talk.

A postcard: "California's Four Seasons"

www.calscene.com

Listening Comprehension

Podcast: NPR Health care Hispanics in the U.S. are likely to be uninsured

Before listening to the recording twice read the following statements. After listening, you must decide which of them are true, false or not in the text.

Statements	true	false	not in the text
1. Many Hispanics are uninsured because of cultural and economic reasons.			
2. Hispanics coming from countries where health insurance is provided are aware of the fact that they have to pay for it in the US.			
3. Health care services for Hispanics should be provided if the health insurance rates are affordable.			
4. In areas where there is increased demand for medical services doctors and nurses of Hispanic origin should work in the clinics and hospitals.			
5. There are no consequences for any American citizen if illegal immigrants are covered by an insurance or not.			
6. The National Hispanic Association is an important advisor of President Obama.			
7. According to the National Hispanic Association undocumented Hispanics who have become legal should have access to medical services.			
8. The US have 7 percent Hispanic doctors and 2 percent Hispanic nurses.			

Working with cartoons

Cartoons are a frequently-used means to express a certain political opinion or attitude. Their function is to epitomize criticism of existing grievances or to make a clear point. The following steps can help you to structure the interpretation of a cartoon.

1. **Source and content**
   Express in a few sentences
   - where the cartoon comes from (e.g. a newspaper, magazine or the Internet)
   - what the cartoon is about or deals with (its theme or subject)
2. **Description**
   Describe all the elements in the cartoon and point out the relationship between them by
   - starting with the foreground and ending with the background
   - carefully describing the features of each of the objects or the outer appearance of the figures (e.g. facial expression, gestures, postures, clothing) and their actions
3. **Message**
   Explain what the cartoonist wants to say or show by examining the caption, the speech bubbles and the picture together (if the cartoon has these features)
4. **Evaluation**
   Give your opinion on the cartoon.

Vocabulary

The cartoon by ... published in	shows/presents depicts deals with/is about	a possible view of/on ... an attitude towards the problem of ...
At first sight the cartoon is	funny/interesting/boring/annoying/confusing	
The first impression of the cartoon is .../What is striking about the cartoon is ...		
The cartoon consists of several pictorial elements. The pictorial elements of the cartoon can easily be distinguished. The first one ...		
In the foreground/background	... is shown/depicted/can be seen.	
The cartoon expresses joy/hate (or other emotions)		
The caption	reads/states/plainly shows that ... is unexpected/forms a contrast to the picture	
The cartoon clearly shows ... It is plain/obvious to see ... The message of the cartoon is ... The cartoonist criticizes man's irresponsible way of ...		

Cartoons about Hispanics

Cartoon 1

Cartoon 2

Cartoon 3

1. Describe the cartoons in detail.
2. What are the cartoonists' messages?

Listening Comprehension

The following speech was delivered by Julián Castro, mayor of San Antonio, TX, at the Democratic National Convention in Charlotte, N.C., on September 4, 2012. He addresses his audience to convince them to officially nominate Barack Obama as candidate to the 2012 presidential election.

You will listen to his speech twice. Before the first presentation you will have five minutes to read all the tasks.

1. **Now listen to the speech for the first time and tick if the statements are true or false.**

statement	true	false
a) Castro's grandmother had to leave her San Antonio school after the fourth grade because her family moved back to Mexico.		
b) In America, everybody has the chance to upward movement.		
c) Previous generations have acted with far-sightedness to improve their children's lives.		
d) Castro's high school classmates in San Antonio did not have the same motivation to succeed in life as his fellow students at Stanford and Harvard university.		
e) The Democratic Party will not support the outsourcing of jobs.		
f) If President Obama is re-elected, America will prosper.		

2. While listening to the speech for a second time, finish the following sentences according to the speech in note form.

1. To be able to give her daughter a better life, Castro's grandmother worked hard as a

   a) ______________________ b) ______________________

   c) ______________________

2. The hard work of former generations made the following things possible:

   a) ______________________ b) ______________________

   c) ______________________

3. The American middle class stands for ______________________

4. To have a chance for a good life, it is essential to get a good ______________________

5. Many immigrants are menaced by ______________________

6. The Democratic Party will not make millionaires even richer by taking the money from ______________________

   ____

7. In the past, America has been able to prevail with ______________________

   ______________________ and ______________________.

3. Castro's speech is a keynote speech, a speech intended to set the underlying tone and summarize the core message of the Democratic National Convention.

   a) Describe the tone of his speech in one word. ______________________
   b) Point out the core message of his speech.

   ____

Julian Castro's DNC Keynote

San Antonio Mayor Julian Castro delivers the keynote address at the Democratic National Convention in Charlotte, N.C., on Tuesday, September 4, 2012

[...] The unlikely journey that brought me here tonight began many miles from this podium. My brother Joaquín and I grew up with my mother Rosie and my grandmother Victoria. My grandmother was an orphan. As a young girl, she had to leave her home in Mexico and move to San Antonio, where some relatives had agreed to take her in. She never made it past the fourth grade. She had to drop out and start working to help her family. My grandmother spent her whole life working as a maid, a cook and a babysitter, barely scraping by, but still working hard to give my mother, her only child, a chance in life, so that my mother could give my brother and me an even better one. [...]

My grandmother didn't live to see us begin our lives in public service. But she probably would have thought it extraordinary that just two generations after she arrived in San Antonio, one grandson would be the mayor and the other would be on his way – the good people of San Antonio willing – to the United States Congress.

My family's story isn't special. What's special is the America that makes our story possible. Ours is a nation like no other, a place where great journeys can be made in a single generation. No matter who you are or where you come from, the path is always forward. America didn't become the land of opportunity by accident. My grandmother's generation and generations before always saw beyond the horizons of their own lives and their own circumstances. They believed that opportunity created today would lead to prosperity tomorrow. That's the country they envisioned, and that's the country they helped build. The roads and bridges they built, the schools and universities they created, the rights they fought for and won – these opened the doors to a decent job, a secure retirement, the chance for your children to do better than you did.

And that's the middle class – he engine of our economic growth. With hard work, everybody ought to be able to get there. And with hard work, everybody ought to be able to stay there – and go beyond. The dream of raising a family in a place where hard work is rewarded is not unique to Americans. It's a human dream, one that calls across oceans and borders. The dream is universal, but America makes it possible. And our investment in opportunity makes it a reality. [...]

And it starts with education. Twenty years ago, Joaquín and I left home for college and then for law school. In those classrooms, we met some of the brightest folks in the world. But at the end of our days there, I couldn't help but to think back to my classmates at Thomas Jefferson High School in San Antonio. They had the same talent, the same brains, the same dreams as the folks we sat with at Stanford and Harvard. I realized the difference wasn't one of intelligence or drive. The difference was opportunity. [...]

And the dream my grandmother held, that work would be rewarded, that the middle class would be there, if not for her, then for her children – that dream was being crushed. But then President Obama took office – and he took action. When Detroit was in trouble, President Obama saved the auto industry and saved a million jobs. Seven presidents before him – Democrats and Republicans – tried to expand health care to all Americans. President Obama got it done. He made a historic investment to lift our nation's public schools and expanded Pell grant so that more young people can afford college. And because he knows that we don't have an ounce of talent to waste, the president took action to lift the shadow of deportation from a generation of young, law-abiding immigrants called *dreamers*.

I believe in you. Barack Obama believes in you. Now it's time for Congress to enshrine

Julián Castro (born 1974) served as Mayor of San Antonio, TX. from 2009 to 2014 and is now the 16th United States secretary of Housing and Urban Development in the cabinet of President Barack Obama.
Democratic National Convention (DNC) a series of conventions held every four years during presidential campaigns. Its goal is to nominate the party's candidate for president and vice president. It is attended by delegates from all fifty U.S. states.
Joaquín Castro twin brother of Julián Castro, has served the United States House of Representatives since 2013, representing Texas's 20th congressional district.
orphan a child whose parents are both dead

Pell grant money the U.S. government provides for students who need it to pay for college.
dreamers illegal immigrants eligible for the DREAM Act (Development, Relief, and Education for Alien Minors), an American legislative proposal for a multi-phase process for undocumented immigrants in the United States that would first grant conditional residency and upon meeting further qualifications, permanent residency.

in law their right to pursue their dreams in the only place they've ever called home: America.

Four years ago, America stood on the brink of a depression. Despite incredible odds and united Republican opposition, our president took action, and now we've seen 4.5 million new jobs. He knows better than anyone that there's more hard work to do, but we're making progress. And now we need to make a choice.

It's a choice between a country where the middle class pays more so that millionaires can pay less – or a country where everybody pays their fair share, so we can reduce the deficit and create the jobs of the future. It's a choice between a nation that slashes funding for our schools and guts Pell grants – or a nation that invests more in education. It's a choice between a politician who rewards companies that ship American jobs overseas- or a leader who brings jobs back home.

to slash to cut, to greatly reduce an amount
to gut to change something by removing some of the most important or central parts

This is the choice before us. And to me, to my generation and for all the generations to come, our choice is clear. Our choice is a man who's always chosen us. A man who already is our president: Barack Obama.

In the end, the American dream is not a sprint, or even a marathon, but a relay. Our families don't always cross the finish line in the span of one generation. But each generation passes on to the next the fruits of their labor. My grandmother never owned a house. She cleaned other people's houses so she could afford to rent her own. But she saw her daughter become the first in her family to graduate from college. And my mother fought hard for civil rights so that instead of a mop, I could hold this microphone. [...]

relay *Staffellauf*

The days we live in are not easy ones, but we have seen days like this before, and America prevailed. With the wisdom of our founders and the values of our families, America prevailed. With each generation going further than the last, America prevailed. And with the opportunity we build today for a shared prosperity tomorrow, America will prevail.

to prevail to be successful in the end

It begins with re-electing Barack Obama. It begins with you. It begins now. *Que dios los bendiga.* May God bless you, and may God bless the United States of América.

Julian Castro's DNC Keynote Address, September 4, 2012; online: http://www.npr.org/2012/09/04/160574895/transcript-julian-castros-dnc-keynote-address [29.01.2015]

Video: www.youtube.com/watch?v=GSvCOCD7UWO

mp3 download: www.npr.org/2012/09/04/160574895/transcript-julian-castros-dnc-keynote-address

Molotov: Frijolero

1. Judging from the band's name and the title of the song (*frijolero* means *beaner* in English) what kind of music do you expect? Speculate on the possible theme of the song.

2. While listening to the song for the first time, note down key words and phrases. In small groups, compare your results and find out the theme the song.

3. While listening to the song for a second time, find the correct order of the following lines.

1	Stay on your side
2	Correcto
3	Ustedes son consumidores
4	I've gotten stared down
5	No me digas beaner
6	Ser un mexicano cruzando la frontera
7	You beaner
8	Nunca inflamos la moneda
9	Now I wish I had a dime
10	Now why don't you look down

4. Read the lyrics and analyze the point of view. Who is speaking to whom? Explain the use of the Spanish and English language.

5. Mediation: Choose one of the following assignments.
   a) Explain in Spanish what the English parts of the song are about to a Spanish friend who does not understand English.
   b) Explain in English what the Spanish parts of the song are about to an American friend who does not understand Spanish.
   c) Explain in German what the song is about to a German friend who understands neither English nor Spanish.

6. Visualize the scene of the Mexican and the border patrol agent talking to each other in a drawing. Write a short text to explain your work.

MOLOTOV: FRIJOLERO

Yo ya estoy hasta la madre
De que me pongan sombrero
Escucha entonces cuando digo
No me llames frijolero
Y aunque exista algún respeto
Y no metamos las narices
Nunca inflamos la moneda
Haciendo guerra a otros países
Te pagamos con petróleo
E intereses nuestra deuda
Mientras tanto no sabemos
Quien se queda con la feria
Aunque nos hagan la fama
De que somos vendedores
De la droga que sembramos
Ustedes son consumidores

Don't call me gringo
You fuckin beaner
Stay on your side
Of that goddamn river
Don't call me gringo
You beaner

No me digas beaner
Mr. puñetero
Te sacaré un susto
Por racista y culero
No me llames frijolero
Pinche, gringo puñetero

Now I wish I had a dime
For every single time
I've gotten stared down
For being in the wrong side of town
And a rich man I'd be
If I had that kind of chips
Lately I wanna smack the mouths
Of these racists
Podrás imaginarte desde afuera,
Ser un mexicano cruzando la frontera
Pensando en tu familia mientras que pasas
Dejando todo lo que conoces atrás
Si tuvieras tú que esquivar las balas
De unos cuantos gringos rancheros
Las seguirás diciendo good for nothing wetback?
Si tuvieras tú que empezar de cero
Now why don't you look down
To where your feet is planted

Frijolero beaner

estoy hasta la madre I'm sick and tired

haciendo guerra a otros paises reference to the US invasion of Iraq in 2003

that goddamn river reference to the Rio Grande

puñetero complicated, spiteful, malicious

pinche Mexican slang: fucking

the wrong side of town reference to the binational metropolitan area of the twin cities of Ciudad Juarez (Chihuahua, Mexico) and El Paso (Texas, USA) on the border

That U.S. soil that makes you take shit for granted
If not for Santa Ana just to let you know
That where your feet are planted would be Mexico
Correcto!

Don't call me gringo
You fuckin beaner
Stay on your side
Of that goddamn river
Don't call me gringo
You beaner

No me digas beaner
Mr. puñetero
Te sacaré un susto
Por racista y culero
No me llames frijolero
Pinche gringo puñetero

soil earth
Santa Ana reference to Antonio de Padua María Severino López de Santa Ana y Pérez de Lebrón (1794 – 1876), a Mexican politician and general who also served as Mexico's president for 22 years. His military failures resulted in Mexico losing a large part of its territory, including the area north of the Rio Grande in 1936.

Die Angst lebt mit: Illegale Einwanderer in den USA (24.11.2012)

[...]

Hector Morales wartet vor einem roten Backsteingebäude in Alexandria, der Einwanderungsbehörde des Bundesstaates Virginia. Für seinen Antrag auf ein US-Aufenthaltsrecht muss Hector seine Fingerabdrücke scannen lassen. Der Mexikaner, der seinen richtigen Namen nicht nennen möchte, ist einer von geschätzt 12 Millionen illegalen Immigranten in den USA. Er ist ein „DREAMer" – ein Träumer. „Dream" bedeutet im Englischen nicht nur Traum, sondern ist auch die Abkürzung für einen Gesetzentwurf. Jugendliche, die illegal ins Land gekommen sind, erhalten dadurch die Chance auf eine Aufenthaltsgenehmigung.

Ein Job, ein Studium oder ein Bankkonto, bisher alles unerreichbare Dinge für den Zwanzigjährigen. „Es gibt nicht viel, was du tun kannst, wenn du illegal hier lebst", sagt er, „ich habe immer das Gefühl, ich stecke einfach fest". Nur wenige seiner Freunde wissen, dass er keine Papiere hat. Am schlimmsten sei die Zeit in der High School gewesen, als alle ihren Führerschein gemacht haben. „Ständig wurde ich gefragt: Und wann bist du dran, wann hast du deine Prüfung?", erzählt er, „dann musste ich mir Lügen ausdenken, damit ich nicht auffalle." Auto fährt Hector trotzdem – ohne Führerschein – und hofft darauf, dass die Polizei ihn nicht anhält.

Hector Morales ist im Alter von neun Jahren mit seiner Familie illegal von Mexiko in die USA eingewandert. „Man kann sich einreden, ein normales Leben zu führen, aber die Angst abgeschoben zu werden, ist einfach immer da", sagt Hector. Mitte des Jahres hatte Präsident Barack Obama eine auf zwei Jahre begrenzte Verfügung erlassen. Gleich im August hat Hector seinen Antrag abgegeben. „Junge Menschen sollten nicht länger mit der ständigen Angst vor Abschiebung leben", teilte der Präsident mit, sie könnten nichts dafür, wenn ihre Eltern sie als Kinder illegal ins Land gebracht hätten. Hector Morales ist eines von ihnen und er erfüllt alle Kriterien, die ihn vor einer Abschiebung bewahren: Seine Eltern brachten ihn als Kind hierher, er lebt seit mehr als fünf Jahren in den USA, er hat sich nicht strafbar gemacht und kann einen Schulabschluss nachweisen. Den braucht Hector, um eine Arbeitserlaubnis zu bekommen. Bisher arbeitet er illegal. Täglich 11 Stunden lang in einem China-Imbiss.

[...]

Die meisten der rund 12 Millionen illegalen Einwanderer sind Latinos, so wie Hector Morales. Sie kommen aus Mexiko, Latein- oder Mittelamerika. Gleichzeitig stellen die Latinos, die legal eingewandert sind, mit rund 50 Millionen Einwohnern die größte und wichtigste Minderheit in den USA. Zwei Drittel der wahlberechtigten Latinos verhalfen mit ihrer Stimme Obama zu einer zweiten Amtszeit. Und das, obwohl unter seiner Regierung die Zahl der Abschiebungen einen neuen Rekord erreicht hat. Laut dem Ministerium für Heimatschutz wurden in dreieinhalb Jahren 1,4 Millionen Menschen aus dem Land gewiesen. Doch die harte Linie seines republikanischen Herausforderers Mitt Romney klang für Einwanderer noch weniger verlockend. Er forderte von ihnen während des Vorwahlkampfes, „sich selbst abzuschieben".

Verena Klein: Die Angst lebt mit: Illegale Einwanderer in den USA, Washingthon DC, 24.11.2012; online: http://www.dw.com/de/die-angst-lebt-mit-illegale-einwanderer-in-den-usa/a-16400313 [29.01.2016]

You get an email from a friend in California who wants to know what Germans know about the situation of young illegal immigrants in the US who were brought there by their parents. You find this article on the Internet and answer your friend.

Blog Entries

June 12, 2009 George

I think this is a great book for people who like a gripping story on a topical subject.
Although there are some weaknesses in the plot "The Tortilla Curtain" by T.C. Boyle is a good read even more than 15 years after its first publication. The problem that it deals with is still relevant – there are still many problems because of illegal immigration especially in the southwest of the US.
Boyle describes how the lives of two couples clash when white Delany Mossbacher hits Mexican Cándido. Delany is the stepfather of Jordan and husband of real estate wizard Kyra. The well-off couple lives on a newly built estate which is protected by a fence and later a wall against coyotes and illegals. Cándido lives in the canyons near Los Angeles with his pregnant young girlfriend América. They are both illegal immigrants who try to make a living by working for very low wages on a day to day basis.
The story is told in alternating chapters – the desperate illegal Mexicans encounter catastrophe after catastrophe whereas the white couple loses more and more their feeling of security. Boyle depicts both sides of the lifestyles that differ extremely and tells his story in a breathtaking style. We as readers learn much about what is going on in the two illegal immigrants' minds and we can feel with them when one mishap after another happens to them up to the birth of a handicapped child. They really are honest people who try to fulfil their American Dream. We also understand why they are forced to leave their country of origin.
Having read the book we feel that there is much left to do to help the victims of illegal immigration and to find a solution to that pressing problem.

August 24, 2006 Susan

I started reading this book because it is a book club choice but I struggled finishing it. It is a really boring story and it is impossible to get interested in the characters although T.C. Boyle is telling us really much about their lives. On the one hand there is the white couple described in a very stereotypical way, on the other hand there are the poor illegal Mexican immigrants who don't get anything right. The book is a bit like the movie "Groundhog Day" – the same thing happens over and over again. Maybe the author intended it that way but I don't see why I should bother reading it.
There is a movie "The Visitor" which deals with the same topic and it is much, much better – the film people got the story right – maybe Boyle should watch it and learn from it.

1. Read the blog entries and summarise what the bloggers praise or criticize.
2. Write your own blog entry stating your opinion of "The Tortilla Curtain". Give reasons.

Musterlösungen zu den Aufgaben der Textausgabe

p. 10: Describe Delaney's feelings after the accident.

Delaney has mixed feelings after hitting the Mexican with his car. He is shocked because he has hurt a human being, feels haunted by the image. He considers himself to be a good person and does not understand how this could happen to him. So he is angry and blames the victim. But he is only worried about the victim after first thinking about the possible damage to his car and the possible consequences for himself.

p. 14: What could be the reason for the man not wanting Delaney to call for medical help?

The Mexican could be an illegal immigrant who fears to be deported or a criminal the police is looking for. He might simply need money.

p. 15: Speculate on how much money Delaney probably gave the victim of the accident.

Individual answers. (Delaney will give him 20 dollars.)

p. 17: What does Delaney tell the reader about the Mexican men in Los Angeles?

- the are all alike: black eyes, mustaches, khaki workshirts, sacklike trousers
- you can find them everywhere
- they have poorly paid jobs that do not require high skills
- they are inconspicuous, discreet
- they are not noticed by the Americans

p. 23: Why does América panic when she realizes that she is lost?

She panics because she is a complete stranger in a frightening neighborhood that she is very unfamiliar with. Since she left her village in Mexico she has never been on her own (without Cándido).

p. 28: Point out the reasons why Cándido does not want América to find a job.

- he does not want to feel useless and old
- he feels guilty because he brought América to the USA, took her from her father
- he is afraid of being separated from her; she might get lost and not find back to their camp
- he fears she could be attacked by men
- he feels responsible and wants to fulfill his duty, wants to be able to provide for his wife
- he wants to keep the promise of a good life he gave her

p 29: Outline the difference between Cándido's first stay in the USA and his situation in the canyon.

During his first stay he had to live in miserable, disgusting places, sharing a bed and an apartment with many illegals; always looking for a job, afraid of the police. In the canyon he feels safe and rather confident about finding a job.

p. 33: Why did Cándido begin to feel he has lost control of his life?

Since he is badly injured and unable to work, América has decided to find a job to be able to buy the food they need. This role of the wife as the breadwinner does not agree with Cándido's traditional Mexican world.

p. 38: Describe a typical morning in the Mossbacher's house in one word.

Possible answers: scheduled, routine, busy, efficient, middle-class, healthconscious, repetitive

p. 48: Where do you think América got the food from?

Individual answers: maybe someone gave it to her, maybe she stole it.

p. 56: Why is it a shock for América to see an American beggar?

She grew up with the idea that all Americans are rich.

p. 61: How does Delaney feel in Arroyo Blanco?

He feels safe, calm, relaxed.

p. 65: Find three words to describe Kyra's attitude towards her job.

Possible answers: ambitious, perfectionist, professional, dedicated, determined to be successful, competitive, demanding, fastidious, profit-oriented, serious, workaholic (?)

p. 75: Can you find a single word to explain América's and Cándido's aggression towards each other in this situation?

Frustration

p. 85: Will América's employer pay her for the extra hours she worked? What do you think?

Individual answers

p. 112: Why does Cándido feel so happy and hopeful?

He is happy and hopeful because after so many days of starving they will have enough food to beat their hunger, América is in a good mood because she has earned money and he is recovering from the accident. He feels also proud because he was able to build a new home for them.

p. 119: What is América afraid of?

América does not trust her boss and is afraid of him finding her rummaging around the bathroom instead of scrubbing buddhas. She even has a bad conscience because she has used the bathroom during working hours.

p. 129: Why is Delaney so tired of the car dealer?

Delaney feels deeply irritated by Kenny Grissom's stupid anecdotes and nonchalant way of dealing with the fact that someone has just stolen Delaney's new car. He is rather annoyed at the constant chatter of this salesman.

p. 138: Why does Kyra think that the situation round the 7-Eleven is bad?

Kyra is very worried about the mass of immigrants hanging around that lot. She thinks that potential buyers of real estate will be put off by so many dark skinned people loitering about. Her customers might want to buy homes not far from the 7-Eleven and they would not appreciate these people.

p. 148: Describe how Cándido feels in this situation.

Cándido feels completely out of his depths at this moment. He realizes that the money he owns cannot help him because he has no idea where he is and where he can find a bus station. The weather is very cold and it starts to rain. He is not used to this kind of climate which makes him feel even unhappier.

p. 151: What makes Cándido run?

It seems as if Cándido follows an instinct that tells him to run away from the officials of immigration. The fear of being caught as an illegal immigrant is deeply ingrained in him and so he follows his first impulse and starts to run off.

p. 159: Why does Cándido hit América?

There are two reasons for him to lose his control and beat his pregnant wife. Firstly, he is rather drunk and so self-control is difficult for him. Secondly, he is very frustrated because he realizes that something very bad happened to América when she made her way through the canyon on her own. Her refusal to talk about whatever has happened makes him even angrier.

p. 166: Do you agree that Dominick Flood is a good guy?

Answers will vary, however, it seems to be hard to imagine that someone who is forced to spend three years under house arrest is really such a good guy. You could argue that getting in trouble because of some wrong investments is no indication of a person being a crook, but a good guy really should not get into conflict with the law.

p. 182: Would you trust this man?

Again answers could vary, however, it is quite apparent that this man is not trustworthy. The way he forces himself on Cándido and América and tries to sell them the idea of sleeping in a nice room that night seems to be too obtrusive. It is understandable that the tired couple is easily persuaded.

p. 202: Describe América's feelings at this point.

América is close to total despair. Not only will they not be able to sleep in a nice bed that night, but after all their money has been stolen they will not be able to find a place to live before her baby is born. Having waited for Cándido for hours and been through a rollercoaster of feelings she is exhausted and desperate.

p. 211: What disadvantage does Delaney see in the construction of the wall?

He cannot walk out of his own yard any more, but will have to hoist himself over the wall.

p. 215: Describe the state América finds herself in and find reasons for this.

América is enthusiastic about something delicious to eat for them. She is very happy and sets to preparing the turkey for dinner and even has a sip of beer.

p. 226: Why does Delaney not feel comfortable at Dominick Flood's party?

He keeps thinking about mishaps that could occur to the food being prepared in his house while the Mexican maid is alone with Jordan. Another thing that worries him is the fear that their Thanksgiving guests will not be hungry anymore after this afternoon party and altogether he cannot really enjoy this type of self-indulgence at this time of the day.

p. 230: To what extent has Kyra changed in the course of the party?

Kyra feels relaxed and enjoys herself at the party. She has prepared everything for their Thanksgiving dinner and now feels that considering her usual workload she deserves to feel at ease at this time. She manages to keep her mind off real estate and easily drifts from group to group talking leisurely.

p. 235: Describe the picture that flashes into Cándido's mind when he realizes the destructive impact of the fire.

Cándido is reminded of an event happening in Arizona when somebody's cigarette had ignited a spill of gasoline from the tank of a tractor and this person burnt to death. Cándido had been watching the horror from up on a lemon tree without being able to do anything.

p. 244: What leads to the tension between Delaney and Kyra?

After Delaney's joke about the state of the turkey Kyra takes her horror and anger about the destructive powers of the fire out on him. Delaney feels unrightly rebuffed and defends himself.

p. 249: State what thoughts and feelings are going through Delaney's mind upon coming back.

Delaney is in a state of confusion for various reasons and some images of the past well up inside him. He almost started a riot because of his suspicion about the Mexican which frightens him. Then he is reminded of an antinuke demonstration he took part in and the exposure to the aggressive behaviour of abortion adversaries when he and his former wife went to an abortion clinic. Back then he was on the side of the people standing up for an issue but now he feels as if he is one of the members of the mob-like crowd shouting and raging without any real evidence.
Furthermore, the odor of charred brush and timber reminds him of the incinerator at his grandmother's apartment and a nearby dump with an umbrella of seagulls.

p. 256: Describe the different feelings Cándido has when he looks at América and his daughter

First, he is shocked to have a daughter because he was expecting to have a son and then it dawns on him that he is finally a father. The next immediate feeling is one of apprehension because he will have to provide something for them to stay alive.

p. 265: Express Kyra's thoughts and state of mind when she is walking around the Da Ros place.

Kyra is in a terrible state when she sees the destruction of the fire. The estate is almost completely gone with only smouldering ash left. Although it is not her own house she has felt a kind of emotional conncection to it. Moreover, she is full of hatred and despise for the two Mexicans that she saw before because she holds them responsible for the cause of the fire. She is outraged at the fact that they cannot be deported for lack of evidence and fears an increase of this kind of events in the future.

p. 275: Which thoughts and feelings are crossing Cándido's mind as he becomes aware of the desperate situation in the shelter?

Several thoughts run through his mind regarding his own persona and his former life: he feels a complete failure because he cannot provide properly for a family and even caused the fire in the canyon. He thinks he is worthless of América and their little daughter and is reminded of his own father who married another woman after his mother had died and who did not love him like his younger siblings. His self-pity culminates in the idea of running away and leaving América and their daughter to themselves.

p. 286: Describe what Kyra is pondering on while driving to pick up Jordan.

For the first time in a long while she is in no hurry to get anywhere and she starts contemplating the nature of her work. There she realizes that most parts of it are not terribly exciting to her any more, but rather boring and that the thrilling bit does not create enough compensation for the rest. She feels a certain pointlessness in her type of job and also ponders the huge amount of time that she has always given to her work.

p. 294: Why is Delaney extremely astonished when he looks at the pictures taken by the tripwire-camera?

Delaney expects to see Cándido in the picture but instead sees Jack Jardine Jr., the son of one of the most militant agitators against the illegal immigration of Hispanics, which is highly ironic.

Glossary of Spanish words, phrases and sentences

a

¿Adónde vas, mi vida?	Where are you going my love?
¿Alguién está aquí?	Is anybody here?
amigo	friend
A sus órdenes.	I'm at your service.
avenidas	avenues
¡Ay caray!	*exclamation:* Hell!

b

barrios	*here:* slums
basureros	people that live on the dump
bota	leather bottle
braceros	temporary agricultural laborers
brinco	jumping
bruja	witch
Buenas	*abbreviation*: Hi.
Buenas noches.	1. Good evening. 2. Good night.
Buenos días.	1. Good morning. 2. Good afternoon.
burrito	soft Mexican pancake with a filling of meat
burro	donkey

c

cabrón	husband who knows that his wife betrays him
caldo	soup
calles	streets
campesino	farmer
cándido	1. white. 2. innocent
cantina	saloon, pub
carnal	*informal:* buddy, friend
cementero	person that is addicted to sniffing cement
centavo	Mexican coin (cent)
cerros	hills
chicano	Mexican American
Chilango	from Mexico city
chiles	chilies
chingado	*Mexican slang:* bastard
chingón	*Mexican slang:* bastard, jerk
cholos	*offensive:* South or Central American Indians
chota	*Mexican slang*: police
ciento ochenta y dos	182
ciento ochenta y uno	181
cinco dólares	five dollars
cocido	stew
conquistadores	conquerors
Como hechas a mano.	Like hand-made.
compadre	*informal:* buddy, friend
compañero	comrade, friend
Comprendo.	I understand.
coyote	1. coyote. 2. refugee smuggler at the border between Mexico and the USA
criada	maid
curandera	witch doctor, Latin American medicine woman

d

dompe	*Spanglish:* dump

e

¿Eres sordo?	Are you deaf?
esquinas	street corners
Estados Unidos	United States

f

favelas	slums
fiesta	festivity, festival
flaco, -a	skinny, slim
frijoles	*Mexican:* beans

g

gabacho	*Mexican, offensive*: foreigner, especially (North) American
gastro	*abbreviation:* gastroen-teritis

gatita	*affectionate:* little cat
giros	remittances
gringo	*offensive:* foreigner, especially (North) American
Gringolandia	*informal, offensive:* land of the foreigners
guantes	gloves
guatón	*informal:* fat man
güero	*Mexican:* blond

h

¿Habla usted español?	Do you speak Spanish?
hamburguesa	hamburger
hijo	son
hijo de la chingada	*Mexican slang:* son of a bitch
hombre	man
huaraches	*Mexican:* rustic sandals
huevos con chorizo	fried eggs with a spicy sausage
huevos hervidos con pan tostado	boiled eggs with toast
huevos rancheros	fried eggs with beans and tomatoes

i

indita	*affectionate:* little Indian
indocumentados	illegal immigrants

l

Laboratorio Médico	Medical Laboratory
ladrón	thief
latinos	people from Latin American countries
linda	pretty
Llame,	*here:* Name is.
loco	crazy
lucha	struggle

m

mala suerte	bad luck
'mano	*abbreviation:* brother, friend
manzanita	camomile
mapache	raccoon
marimba	instrument like a xylophone
Me llamo América	My name is América
mendigos	beggars
mercado	market
mi amor	my love
Migra	*abbreviation:* immigration officers, U.S. border patrol
mijo	*abbreviation:* my son
milagro de milagros	miracle of miracles
mi vida	*here:* my love
mojados	wetbacks; illegal immigrants
mole	dark Mexican sauce
momento	moment
muchacho	young man
Muchísimas gracias.	Thank you so much.
muy gacho	*Mexican slang:* very bad

n

nachos	hot corn chips with spicy melted cheese
niñitos	*affectionate:* little kids
niños	kids
No lo necesito.	I don't need him.
No problema.	No problem.
No quiero un matasanos	I don't want a doctor.
el Norte	the North, the USA
norteamericanos	North Americans
novelas	novels

p

paisano	compatriot, fellow countryman
pandillero	gang member
papacito	daddy
Para las manos.	For the hands.
patrón	boss
pelirojo	red-haired
pendejo	*Mexican slang:* bastard, jerk
pinche	*Mexican slang:* fucking
pinche puta	fucking whore
poco	a little
Ponlos allá.	Put them over there.
pulque	alcoholic drink made of agaves

q

¿Qué onda?	*informal:* What's up? What's happening?
¿Qué pasa?	What's happening?
querido	honey; darling, love
¿Quieres joder conmigo?	*slang*: Do you want to fuck me?
¿Quieres trabajo?	Do you want to work?
Quiero trabajar.	I want to work.

r

ranchera	music typical of Northern Mexico
rebozo	shawl
reinas del cine	movie stars
rico	rich
romeritos	rosemary
rubio	blond
ruca	*Mexican slang:* sexy

s

sabe	know
salsa	sauce
señor	Mister
señora	Misses
señorita	Miss
serape	a long blanket, often brightly colored, worn by Mexican men
serranos	spicy Mexican sausages
Si dios quiere.	If God wants it this way.
simpático	*here:* nice
socorro	help
sombreros	hats
supermercado	supermarket

t

taquería	snackbar that sells tacos (Mexican pancakes filled with meat, tomatoes, lettuce etc.)
tarjeta verde	Green Card
terminado	finished
tortilla	a round, thin Mexican pancake, usually eaten hot with a filling of meat etc.
trabaja	he (she) works
tragafuegos	firebreather
turistas	tourists

v

vago	bum, tramp
Vamos.	Let's go.
vías	small streets
vida	life
viejo	old
Virgen Sagrada	the holy Virgin

y

¿Y tú?	And you?
Yo soy.	I am.

Bildquellenverzeichnis

S. 3 (oben, groß): public domain, source: Environmental Protection Agency, http://water.epa.gov/infrastructure/wastewater/mexican/index.cfm; S. 3 (oben, klein): © RFJohner/F1online Bildagentur; S. 3 (unten, groß): © Les Stone/Les Stone/Corbis; S. 3 (unten, klein): © PatrickPoendl/istockphoto; S. 6: © Adam Berry/Getty Images; S. 43 (alle): Víctor Prischtt; S. 44 (beide). S. 45 (beide): Franz-Josef Domke/Verlagsarchiv Schöningh; S. 112: Verlagsarchiv Schöningh; S. 124: www.calscene.com; S. 127 (oben): © Cartoonarcadio Esquivel/caglecartoons.com; S. 127 (unten): © Steve Greenberg; S. 128: *Nick Anderson Editorial Cartoon* used with the permission of Nick Anderson, the Washington Post Writers Group and the Cartoonist Group.

Sollte trotz aller Bemühungen um korrekte Urheberangaben ein Irrtum unterlaufen sein, bitten wir darum, sich mit dem Verlag in Verbindung zu setzen, damit wir eventuell erforderliche Korrekturen vornehmen können.